Coming Up
For Air

D. SEAN

DSEANBOOKS.COM

RAINDUST

RAINDUST LLC
P. O. Box 669281
Marietta, GA 30066
raindustllc.com

Published in the United States
by Raindust LLC

ISBN-13: 978-0-983-4034-0-1
ISBN-10: 0983403406
Library of Congress Cataloging-in-Publication Data
Sean, D. Coming Up For Air/ by D. Sean

This book is dedicated to my three biggest fans:

God; for always calling my bluff

Lisa; for knowing and telling me I could do this even before I did

And finally, Daddy; for being a constant encouragement to my dreams, regardless of their insanity.

One

The heat of the sun warmed my skin as I reclined on a lounge chair. I took a deep breath and closed my eyes. Salty air tickled my nose while an unexpected giggle escaped my lips. A deep rumble vibrated beneath me, creeping upward as it progressed. It began just above the base of my spine, making a deliberate ascent that shook its way up and beyond my shoulders. Then came an eruption of laughter, a soothing baritone. The familiar sound swaddled me with a tangible strength, a simmering that made me feel warm and comforted, while also sending a chill through me. Goose bumps on my exposed flesh.

In the next moment, I joined the chorus of laughter, making harmony with the sweet outpouring. Opening my eyes, I gazed at an endless sea of green and blue, boasting spectacular hues. It went on for miles making me wonder if someone had measured the distance, the depth. I tried to guess at what it might be but the possibilities and equations sent my mind into overload. A faint little migraine at my temples. Sad to say, but math had never been my strength. I refocused, hoping the headache would disappear. Nearby, the rolling tide lapped at the shore. Among tiny granules of sand, evidence of marine life lay strewn about as treasure for someone's keepsake.

That vibration I'd felt resonated beneath me again and color splashed into the white spaces of an incomplete picture. Muted sound faded in like a crescendo, as if I'd been dancing between radio stations and had, at last, tuned in to single frequency. Sounds became clear: raucous laughter, crashing waves, clanging dishes, myriads of conversation, and music. Dancing music, ubiquitous music, reggae music. I felt it around me like a pair of strong arms, its rapture tangible. To prove this point to myself, I extended my fingertips in an attempt to touch it, to feel the rapture. Taut, honey-colored skin, warmed my fingers as I grazed the smooth, soft covering of muscle which looked as though someone had molded it from clay. A barbed wire tattoo looped its way around one arm.

Satisfied, I looked down to find myself seated between large thighs and a pair of huge feet planted in the sand. Then I focused on my dainty toes, stained a vibrant shade of green—my favorite color. I pulled my gaze upwards, imbibing small details of my body and his. I took note of my copper-tinted skin, shiny from being slathered with oil and his, almost void of any at all. I wore a green checkered bikini, tied at either hip, and as if for punctuation, a noticeable mole sat right above my left hipbone. His brown, plaid trunks complimented the color of his skin, his thighs hidden underneath them. Our hands lay entwined, resting on my stomach, each flashing a glimmer of shiny metal on one finger; wedding rings. The vibration shook me again, his laughter filled my ears.

"Echo. Echo!"

I shifted at the sound of my name.

"Yeah," I answered, distracted.

I'd been reclined against Skylar's massive torso for a time, feeling little tremors every time he spoke and large ones when he laughed. The person who'd called my name, however, had not been Skylar. It had been Kennedy's voice who'd called out to me. We'd been the best of friends since we were eleven years old, translating to almost twenty years of friendship. That still sounded strange to my ears, despite its the truth.

"Have you heard anything we've said in the last few minutes?" Without waiting for me to answer, she continued, "You were laughing one minute and gone the next. What, are we boring you? If I didn't know any better, I'd think you were ignoring us. Are you okay?"

"Oh, yeah. I'm fine," I said. She and her husband, Bryant, were also occupying a single lounge chair.

"Fine? Just fine? Fine is how you describe a day at

work! How could you just be fine," she air quoting the last word. "In a place like this? This is when you use words like, spectacular and fabulous! Not fine!"

I had to agree, but didn't concede aloud. This was on the top of my list of favorite vacation spots. The Jamaican sun—or maybe the rum—seemed to have mystical powers. I reached my arms up behind me, grasping for Skylar but I came away empty. I continued my futile search and, all at once, I became aware of the heat and the sweat on my skin. I continued to reach out in various directions for anything, anyone I could feel. Panic rose as my fruitless efforts dragged on. A loud smack startled me.

———◄

I snapped my head up from a sweat-soaked pillow. Sunlight streamed with graceful intent through the floor to ceiling windows that served as walls throughout most of our fourteenth-floor condo. The brightness felt like an insult, an expletive to my dilated pupils. I panted and peeled plastered curls from my damp face. Propped up on one elbow, while most of my dark hair lay strewn across two pillows, my eyes made their way to the floor. Though my eyes were only half adjusted to the morning sun, I saw my cell phone. It lay in three pieces, covered, chunked and scattered, the source of my rude awakening. My phone had fallen, or maybe I'd knocked it down; I couldn't be sure. I'd had it for just a few days, but I wasn't surprised that it was already in bits. I didn't get up right away, made no effort to put Humpty Dumpty back together again. Instead, I fell back against the bed with a heavy sigh, covering my face with the driest pillow. One would think I'd grown accustomed to this by now, these dreams of tropical vacations, saturated with love and laughter. It wouldn't be such a nightmare if not for the fact that this was the 532nd morning in a row I'd awakened to an empty bed, clammy, cold sheets, and the realization that the husband that I'd dreamt of was dead. That word still made me cringe. Whether speaking of a person, a dream, or a goldfish, my reaction remained the same.

I lay in bed, bare, except for a delicate piece of jewelry gracing my left ankle, a gift from Skylar. Hanging from my anklet, a tiny silver basket glimmered in the sun. He would always say he needed an extra place to put all the happiness I gave him. At the time, I thought it cheesy, although still cute, but I wondered how much extra he could fit into such a miniature basket. Now all I wished to hear his lines, lame excuses and earnest reasoning for all that he'd do.

Enough! I thought. My night had been bad enough without the added, self-imposed torture of my longing, heaping more coals onto an ever-burning fire. I catapulted myself out of bed and almost stepped on the hard edges of the phone pieces. Scooping up the disseminated parts, I reassembled the unit without thinking. It wasn't the first time I'd smashed my phone, and I'd bet my right boob it wouldn't be the last.

Standing in my curtain-less window, I stared out

at the bay and the halo of fog surrounding the peaks of the bridge and mountains in the distance. I waited as the phone powered up and went through several alarm tones, alerting me to new messages. Most of them had come during the night. Most callers knew to leave a message after a certain hour. Skylar and I kept the relentless ritual of turning off our cell phones when we crossed the threshold to our home. We didn't want to allow anyone to infringe on our precious time together. Oh, how precious it was. He seemed aware of how short a life could be, as though he were preparing me for a life without him all along. It seemed he knew he wouldn't always be here to take care of me or plan for the things I'd never think of. It had been almost eighteen months since his death and I still operated as though he were here.

All his belongings remained where he'd left them. Skylar, a meticulous man, kept things quite clean—for a guy. Disorder had no place except when he set fire to my body with his. Then, passion overruled any objections logic could make. Plenty of mornings we'd wake and wonder what force had ripped through our place while we slumbered, even as memory and all the evidence pointed guilty fingers at us. There's no telling who else pointed guilty fingers at the couple on the fourteenth floor. We'd never put window treatments on any of our walls of windows. Hand and body prints mottled the otherwise invisible walls, a true and undeniable testament to what had gone on behind closed doors and open windows.

Both of us loved and grew up in the city, I in

Seattle and he in Boston. So when it came to purchasing property, there was no argument to what type of property we wanted. We moved into this ultra-modern, state-of-the-art—whatever that meant—building with its shiny finishes and bucket full of amenities. Long, sleek hallways led to numbered doors on every floor with glossed and sealed concrete floors. Having such low-maintenance floors worked well for me, a lot less carpet to destroy. Our condo had few furnishings, instead, it showcased smooth, reflective metals. We enjoyed free space, so we chose not to fill it with bulky furniture, opting for a breakfast bar in lieu of a formal dining area since we never had "formal" company or "formal" meals for that matter.

The bedroom contained the essentials: a bed with nightstands situated upon each side, nothing else. The vacancy between the "his and hers" walk-in closets was, perhaps, meant to hang a flat screen television, but not in our home. We chose to focus on more entertaining activities, which for the two of us was never in short supply.

I stared out the window as I waited for my phone to finish beeping, buzzing, and chirping. Ironically, the penetrating quiet of the room pulled me from my reverie. Listening to my messages, I paid attention to the one that mattered most, which came from Kennedy. She said we had plans today and she was on her way to my house. That had been twenty minutes ago. *Crap!* I hadn't the slightest idea what those "plans" were, which would make getting dressed that much more challenging. I didn't want to call her because I'd have to admit I'd forgotten. What could it be? Clueless me. Not far from the everyday, it seemed. I scampered across the polished oak floors to the bathroom and turned on the shower. Within seconds, steam scaled the glass box, filling the large bathroom. Well, at least I'll save valuable seconds by not having to undress.

I showered, not even taking time to enjoy the heat of the spray on my tight muscles. Reserving no time for languor, I washed my hair and hopped out, much too soon for my liking. I almost slipped as I dashed to my closet. Years of klutziness had sharpened my reflexes, and I caught myself on the doorjamb. As I stared at the pattern of the wood that had almost imprinted my face, I remembered how Skylar had insisted we get wood, instead of concrete in the bedroom, convinced I'd break a bone or that he'd break me with our shenanigans. I couldn't be more grateful. It amazed me how much foresight he'd had.

Still unsure of how to dress for an unknown event, I decided to wear a pair of almost dressy jeans—if such a thing existed—and a sleeveless, cerulean top with an asymmetrical hem and vertical cinch up the side seam. It's a learned behavior that took some training to dress to flatter rather than flatten my figure. Being the uncommon combination of German and Jamaican gave me plenty to both admire and contend with. My hair, when left on its own, dried in long, loose tresses. My hazel eyes, a compliment to my melanin-tinted flesh, also caused shock when they'd transform into a fierce and undeniable shade of green, according to my mood. They were more often than not green in the presence of Skylar. At five feet, five inches tall with more than just a handful of breasts, thick waist and protruding bottom, Skylar would call me his second helping because a plateful just wasn't enough to contain me.

I donned a pair of tan and turquoise espadrilles and as I bent over to tie the colored ribbons around my ankles, I tried to think of something decent to do with my hair. Looking at my thick mane of damp curls, cascading to the floor, offered no inspiration. Treading back towards the bathroom, extra cautious not to slip again, I sat down on my side of the double vanity. I had no time to spare for complicated "DOs," so I decided to pull my hair into a tight chignon. Skylar, flat out hated this hairdo. He said it made me look uptight, the exact opposite of my personality. With thoughts of him, I left a few tendrils out of the slick ponytail. Afterwards, I rummaged through the shallow drawer until I found what I'd been searching for, a small tube of mascara. I unscrewed the top with confidence but pulled out a warped brush. Bits of dried black clumps dropped onto the marble counter.

"Ugh! Didn't I just buy this stuff?" I asked aloud, slamming the drawer closed and yanking open another. "Aha! I knew it!"

There sat a little black bag of cosmetics with the receipt still sitting atop the merchandise. Grabbing the new tube of mascara, I pulled out the brush and dragged it along my eyelashes. Putting the makeup on forced me to look into eyes I didn't recognize anymore. When was the last time I'd seen any green in my eyes at all? I could't recall. Not even a hint, not a speck of the once frequent green. Thankful the task took very little time, I finished up and moved on to my lips, coating them in a light gloss.

Satisfied enough with the results, I grabbed a small tote from the closet. While I filled it with random items, including my phone, I heard a quick rap at the door. I made no move to answer, because I knew Kennedy was on the other side. Next, I should've heard the key moving into the lock but instead, I heard another knock on the door and then a voice. I made my way to the door, wondering why Kennedy hadn't just used her key as she always did. Before I'd even turned the doorknob, I began my spiel:

"Kennedy, where is your key? I swear if you—" I cut my rant short. My best friend wasn't at the door.

"Delivery," the stranger in a brown uniform said in a flat voice. Ignoring my tirade, he jabbed the electronic notepad at me. "Please sign."

I took it and signed *Echo G. Wells*, dumbfounded, not that he noticed or cared. He handed me the nondescript, tan box void of any labels and about the size of a half-gallon carton of ice cream. As soon as my fingers were on it, he turned and walked away without another word or side glance. Perplexed, I stood there for a moment. All packages went to or through the concierge. At best, the mailman shoved them into reserved lockers near the community mailboxes. Why was this hand-delivered? Furthermore, why hadn't Gary buzzed me with a warning or ask permission? It wasn't uncommon that we...er, I received packages. An outpouring of them came following the accident. People still, even after all this time, sent gifts. Everyone loved Skylar and, by extension, they loved me too. All the things we'd ordered come much too late; I placed the package on the kitchen counter. Later, I'd toss it with all the other unopened packages in our "spare" room.

Dismissing the odd delivery, I went to the fridge. Its stainless steel gleamed as though polished moments ago. Skylar hated having fingerprints or smudges marring the metal's beauty. I poured myself a glass of milk to stave off nausea. Before I'd raised it to my lips, I heard two short raps on the door and then the key unlocked the door as I'd expected earlier. Like crimson sunshine, Kennedy burst in.

"Good morning!" she sang. "It's still morning, right? You know I can hardly keep track of the time. What time is it anyway? Am I late? Whatever, doesn't matter. How are you, hun? What's this?"

Can I speak now? I wanted to ask, but Kennedy had always been this way, a living, breathing run-on sentence. The last question she'd asked referred to the package. I wasn't sure which question to answer first, or if she wanted an answer to any of them. While she rambled, I drank my milk, giving her the moments she needed to pause and, perhaps, breathe. I often wondered if she took breaths between thoughts or sentences, for I never heard the intake.

Kennedy Keigle. A statuesque five feet, nine inches tall with billowing, somewhat muted crimson-colored hair. Not so mute in the sunshine, as evident now. Her head of long, loose, coltish curls, were a startling contrast to her eyes, which were a pale shade of blue. A tiny pointed nose, pinched at the tip and thin lips painted red—today. She'd always been a bit wiry, but since marrying Bryant six years ago, she'd filled to a healthy build, making her look more like a model and less like someone I wanted to incessantly feed. She wore a red pencil skirt with a black ruffled top and peep-toe pumps.

Still skating on the hope that Kennedy would reveal this mystery day to me, I finished my milk without answering any questions and turned to rinse the dish in the sink. Kennedy came into the kitchen, wrapped her arms around my neck and planted a ruby-red kiss on my right cheek. Thank goodness for smudge-free lipstick.

"Hey, sweet thang!" She smacked me full on the bottom as if this were normal. I suppose it was...for her. "What's this?" she asked again.

This time she waited for an answer as she thrummed her manicured nails on top of the unopened box. The query hadn't been rhetorical.

"Oh, that came a few minutes before you showed up. I thought you'd lost your key again, already letting you have it as I opened the door. Poor guy never saw it coming."

"He came to your door? Did you approve that? Why didn't Gary just take it? Why is this so special? Are you going to open it or just throw it in the back with the others?"

Again, unsure of which question to oblige, I exercised random selection.

"I have no intention of opening it. Just throw it in the pile, would you?"

She clunked her way to the other room as I put away the glass that I'd washed and dried. I grabbed my keys and feigned excitement.

"Ready? Let's go." Kennedy breezed by, taking my hand on the way out. The smell of her light perfume and shampooed mingled together, creating an olfactory bouquet.

She swung me out into the hallway and locked the door so fast, for a moment, I thought she'd never removed the keys from the lock. We arrived on the first floor, and seeing Kennedy's car made me glad I'd pulled my hair back. She had opted to drive her brand spanking new Audi R8 convertible. A candy-coated, clean enough to lick, red Spyder something-point-something. The numbers elude me. I never did understand why manufacturers named their cars with numbers. That's a surefire way for me to forget. I must admit, it was a beautiful car, not that I expected anything less out of the one and only Mrs. Kennedy Keigle-Ascot. Had this thing even been released to the public yet? I mean, besides hers. This woman had a keen way of acquiring whatever she wanted. Be it material or otherwise, secret or known, open to the public or private engagement, on the road or in this case, recently approved prototype. How she did it, I'll never know, even when witness to it.

She walked with a body language that said: "Ta-Da!" though her lips never moved. Had I not known her or not been privy to her ostentation, I would have been wide-eyed and slack-jawed. Instead, I froze on the step leading into the small lot. She stood there, a firm grip on my hand, no doubt, hoping I wouldn't hyperventilate, as I had so many times before. Cars still frightened me…even my own. In my head, I saw a flash of crashing windows and slow moving air bags, breaking free of their confines. I ran my finger along the length of my right thigh.

"I'll drive reasonably. I promise," she said, still beaming her sunshine. "Come on, honey. Hop in. This thing is so new that if you listen hard enough, you can still hear the cow's moo coming from the leather!"

I laughed and moved with her a little easier, losing my horrid vision to her mounting babble. Without a breath, she pulled me along, going on about the channels she'd clicked to get a car that hadn't even had a price that included U.S. currency yet. We hopped in and she eased away from the curb and slipped into traffic.

The California sun beamed its relentless heat, but the swirling breezes made it bearable. It helped that I lived rather close to the San Francisco Bay, where the temperature could be quite a few degrees cooler than the forecast called for. Thinking of that now, I wished I'd brought a sweater. I had no idea how long we'd be out, and the night air would bring a guaranteed chill. I looked over at Kennedy and realized she'd never stopped talking. I hadn't heard any of what she'd said, so I made an effort to listen.

"...so we still have to make a stop, because I never went out to get a gift. Did you? Of course you didn't, otherwise you would've gotten one for me too. And seeing as you're empty-handed, well that's proof positive..." she chattered.

Gift? What gift? Whose party? A birthday, an anniversary? Dang it! Why couldn't I remember? What's today's date? I thoughts, as if that would help me recollect.

"I don't even know what to get. What do you think? Pink, blue, yellow, who knows? Useful or playful? Maybe we could go in together on a..." she continued.

What the hell was she talking about? Bewilderment must be my theme for the day. It seemed I couldn't figure anything out. I had more questions than answers but refused to ask...and I called her obstinate.

Moments later, we pulled up in front of a store with the cutest name: *Giggle*. The name itself made me smile, until I realized what type of merchandise it sold. Loud snaps went off in my head as all the pieces began to click into place. The air stifled and my lungs started to constrict.

"We're going to a baby shower!" I huffed, breathless.

"Yes, you said you were okay with this. You said you'd be able to handle it." A slow realization came into her eyes and spread to her face. "You forgot, didn't you?"

Another question rhetorical? I couldn't figure, too busy trying to breathe. She withdrew a paper bag from her larger-than-what's-ever-necessary purse and handed it to me with a look of ambivalence. I could read the emotions, both sympathy and agitation. April 17th! It's April 17th, the day of Amber's baby shower. Amber Mathieson, wife of Jeff Mathieson of the Mathieson & Wright Law Firm in Calabasas. These were heavy investors in K. Keigle Designs, Kennedy's interior design company. Her baby, her livelihood, her life revolved around what she'd created for herself.

She'd asked me months before to attend with her, thinking she'd be unable to bear it alone. Babies, pregnant women, both made her nervous and a little queasy, if she told the truth but she wouldn't dare miss it after all the business and referrals they'd given her. She'd shrouded their massive office in furnishings and tapestries from places I stammered to pronounce, let alone find on a map. She had also decorated and redecorated their homes in Beverly Hills and Calabasas, not to mention several vacation homes and a plethora of client referrals. They were having their first child.

Our baby would have been rounding six months about now, a first for both Skylar and me. We hadn't even known we'd wanted a baby, until that stick changed color. Skylar couldn't contain himself but, a month later, I still had not quite processed that we were going to be parents. By the time I'd accepted the idea and joined the party and preparations, they had both been torn from my hold. However, not before Skylar had had the chance to order a mountain of things, including furniture that we wouldn't have needed for at least another six months. Boxes still arrived on occasion, things that he'd purchased despite being on backorder for months.

Pinpricks bombarded my heart, and I fought the urge to sob all over Kennedy's mooing seats. Instead, I took a moment—or twelve—to train my thoughts elsewhere. Somewhere that didn't hurt as much. I concentrated on the vacancies of my mind, forcing my thoughts to get lost in the nothingness of unoccupied space. It's the one place that didn't include lost loves and lives. It's where I went to paint something new. A blank canvas of white, awaiting my ready brush. After a while, my breathing returned to normal and I felt the strain in my face dissipate. Kennedy hadn't moved, she just held my hand, patient as always. Had she ever let it go? I don't know if Kennedy will ever know how much I love her.

"I can do this alone if you're not up for it, hun. It's just a stupid baby party."

The way her face contorted when she said "baby" amused me. I felt the corners of my mouth turn up. She burst into laughter, knowing full well she couldn't stomach this by herself. Hell, she thought morning sickness was contagious! Kennedy would wait until she knew I had drunk my customary glass of milk, before crossing my path. I can't figure out how she'd always come at the perfect time. I joined the laughter and opened the door. With a squeeze and gentle tug on my hand, she sat me back down. She gave me a look that begged the question "Are you sure?" It's wonderful, all the things you can say without uttering a word. I affirmed with a minuscule nod. To an onlooker, it appeared as though we were just staring at each other, but we often made deals that way. Ever since we were kids, we'd communicated around everyone else's understanding, including our parents.

We walked into *Giggle* hand in hand, drawing a peculiar look from the sales clerk. It didn't help that my free hand rested on my flat abdomen. The focus of her eyes there brought it to my attention and I removed my hand. All of this in a matter of seconds and completely over Kennedy's head.

"Hi," she chimed. "We need a gift for a shower." She avoided the "B" word, which caused me to chuckle. She gave my hand a little squeeze and continued without missing a beat. "What do you recommend? What's most popular? Nothing cheap please. I need a special gift, not something seven other people have already given them. No need to break the bank either. Furniture would be great, but as you can see," she gestured to the car outside, "I'm not driving a vehicle meant to haul anything but ass! So let's see what you've got."

The clerk looked confused and smoothed back one side of her mussed hair. Most people had a hard time figuring out what to make of Kennedy at first impressions.

The plain-looking woman with wide hips, wider thighs and an expansive midsection looked at Kennedy and then to me.

"Miss," I said, hoping to eradicate the dumb stare fixed on her face. "Can you start with the most popular small furniture choices, please? Something in a small box."

"Uh, certainly," she stammered.

Forty minutes later, we decided to get a swanky highchair. The cost: $400. Kennedy doesn't do frugal or reasonable. I, on the other hand, do. We bought a greeting card and put the certificate inside, with a picture stating what we'd bought—and by "we," I mean Kennedy.

My insides fluttered the closer we got to our destination. I knew we were close because Kennedy reminded me every so many miles. As we drove along the coast, the air ran wild, invisible fingers through her hair. It seemed to leave red streaks in our wake. I closed my eyes and laid my head back on the headrest, trying to will the insects in my belly to sleep or die. I preferred they die. A tune danced around my ears but I wasn't certain if it came from the radio or Kennedy's singsong voice. I didn't care enough to open my eyes and find out.

For a moment in time, I saw Skylar. His oval-shaped face smiling at me from his six foot, two inch frame. Remarkable gray eyes filled with laughter, as though privy to some inside joke that no one else could hear. He had a wide nose and lips that begged me to kiss them, and we kissed often. So much, in fact, I often wondered if it were my fault that his lower lip was plumper than the upper. He loved when I tugged at it with my teeth. Skylar had strong shoulders, a thicker-than-average midsection and brawny legs. I enjoyed the fact that he didn't have a swimmer's build or standard athletic physique and reveled in the soft contours and rounded edges of his body.

I felt myself smile and the rampant wind died down to a breeze. What song is she singing? I thought. Blinking into awareness and watching Skylar's image swirl away, I saw what had to be our destination. Those blasted insects in my stomach hadn't died as I'd wished, but at least they'd taken a nap. Now, they had resumed with abundant life.

We inched along a lengthy driveway. One car among many. The melody I'd heard came from the estate we approached. This was no run-of-the-mill baby shower. This was more like a baby downpour. I looked over at Kennedy who seemed unfazed by my aloofness. Maybe she thought I'd been napping.

At last, we'd made it to the center of the circular driveway, where valets stood, waiting to park our car. The gleam in one kid's eyes sparkled as we pulled in, his excitement obvious. He looked gleeful when we stopped in front of him while his coworkers exchanged looks of jealously as they eyed the showpiece of a car.

"If I find dirt on the wheels or dust on the paint..." Kennedy began, speaking to the zealous boy holding her door open.

She didn't bother finishing her sentence, instead, she drilled a long, formidable glare into this child's eyes, enough to yank the excitement right from his lungs. He expelled an audible *whoosh* as his lips parted, but said nothing. He just stood stock still, maybe more frightened by the tranquil nonchalance in which she spoke than the words themselves.

"As a matter of fact, hold your breath while you're in it," she added.

His mouth closed and the rapid rise and fall of his chest, clear and present a moment before, vanished. *Poor kid*, I thought. Kennedy did this for sport. She didn't care that much.

After we got out of the car, ushers led us into the foyer of the 1920's estate. It had been remodeled and restored beyond its original beauty and, of course, decorated by Kennedy. This I knew, for I had held several events at the estate myself. It happened to be one of my favorite venues and a favorite of many of my clients. Being an event planner meant research and, more often than not, repeats. Kennedy and I had worked together a time or few. We were like unofficial business partners, often collaborating on projects. Clients loved us as a team, and the results were phenomenal and unmatched—their words, not ours. The estate had old world charm, new world conveniences and the undistorted view of the coastline didn't hurt either.

We shuffled out the imported French doors into the yard, where a large tent had been erected. The music grew louder and more distinct. Tchaikovsky, Pas De Deux from the Nutcracker. I'd read somewhere that classical music enhanced brain function in infants. The Mathiesons must have read that too. Either that or they were genuine lovers of classical music as I am. Before we had descended the few stairs leading onto the acreage, I saw Mrs. Mathieson making her way through an opening between her guests. I had no time to process this or prepare my psyche for the eye-full of belly coming straight at us. Amber Mathieson, the woman with a frame so tiny she didn't even look sturdy enough to carry a large handbag, let alone the giant baby that caused her belly to protrude a foot in front of her. Maybe that's an exaggeration, but it looked like it.

Her blond bob, parted down the middle, framed her dainty face. Wire-rimmed glasses rested on her nose and a diamond, I could see prisms in even from a distance, weighed down her finger. Kennedy matched Amber's enthusiastic approach as we walked closer to meet the waddling woman. The two had become quite fond of each other over time.

"Kennedy, you're here!" Amber kissed her cheek.

"As if I wouldn't be! You know I—" Kennedy began.

"Thank goodness!" Amber interrupted Kennedy's pending chatter. *Good move!* I thought. She wouldn't get a word in otherwise. "I'm in desperate need of a diversion. I've needed to use the restroom for much too long. Walking is enough of a chore without stopping to talk every few feet and with a full bladder no less."

Amber turned and looked at me as though I'd just walked up. A long silence followed, at least long to me. Had my face turned blue from lack of oxygen or green with envy?

"Echo?" Amber said.

Was she asking me my name? My head snapped up to her eyes, having been locked on her swollen abdomen.

"Amber, I'm sorry. I just—" I scrambled to recover. "You are too tiny for such a belly. You look great!"

Kennedy didn't help at all, she appeared to be almost as awkward as I did. Thank heavens Amber was quick on her feet.

"Thanks, but I'm huge. It's good to see you. It feels like such a long time since I've laid eyes on you. This is a little inappropriate," she looked around. "But I really have to use the restroom. Please, ladies, wait here for me."

She scampered away as fast as her swollen feet would carry her. I would have offered her a much warmer greeting, but my fear of touching her had overwhelmed. As though touching her anywhere on her pregnant body would send me crumbling to bits right there on the manicured lawn.

"We can slip this card under the bathroom door and dash out of here faster than she can pull up her underwear. What do you think?" Kennedy looked back towards the house. As much as we both wanted to put that plan into motion, we knew we couldn't. I let out an uneasy giggle.

"You won't be dashing anywhere in that get up," I teased, looking her up and down while waving a condescending finger at her. "Besides, you know I'd probably do a face plant into that marble floor, a tragic getaway."

"We have to loosen up. Do they serve drinks at these things? I'm not talking about punch either. I need something with a punch. What is taking her so long?" Kennedy writhed with impatience.

I'm sure she wished this could be one of our "band-aid" parties. Successfully pulled off and dismissed right away. I know I wished for it but found comfort in knowing this wouldn't be a 'normal' shower with goofy, infant-themed games and cheap door prizes no one wanted to win.

Kennedy took a visible breath, I'm sure in preparation for another complaint. Looking beyond her, I could see Amber's silver, beaded tank top glittering in the sunlight. She stepped through the door and made her way back to us. She looked chic, but simple in a pair of plain black leggings and flat shoes. She had also refreshed her make-up, donning an almost nude shade of lipstick and adding a little blush to her cheeks. She walked with a lot less urgency. Kennedy turned around, glanced at Amber and then back to me. She looked relieved and a little sick. I needed to get her a drink, fast and maybe one for me too.

"You ladies want a drink?" Amber asked as though she had been spying my thoughts.

Kennedy and I had had time to regroup, and we were now in "event" mode. We had separate personas for our events. Personas that allowed us to meld with the personalities of our clients and their guests. She had given the subtle sign, just before Amber returned. My demeanor and posture changed on cue, and I brightened to at least a dim bulb. Why hadn't I thought of this before? It would've made that first moment with Amber a lot less awkward. A flash of relief crossed both our faces as Amber listed all the drinks *she* couldn't have.

"We have champagne, beer, wine—red and white—and a full bar of whatever cocktail you'd like."

By now, we were walking across the expansive lawn, passing the small orchestra, the source of the music I'd recognized earlier. We were all walking with more confidence. Kennedy and I, because we had on our "business faces" and Amber because she no longer had a full bladder, weighted down by an enormous baby. Amber walked and talked, but not without effort. Her labored breathing made me nervous and I wished she'd slow her pace, for my sake. She pointed out people and named them and their professions or relations. Some I recognized, others were new. This had become a networking party. It was the best way to get through this wretched "shower." Now I had trouble with the "B" word. Dammit, Kennedy!

She'd given me her disease.

Kennedy, after a drink, seemed more at ease. So did I. We worked the room—tent, rather. After a time, Kennedy and I decided that we'd been more than cordial and searched for a graceful way to escape. Amber entertained a small group of her many guests. Instead of interrupting her we found her husband, Jeff, to say our goodbyes. He stood to one far corner of the tent, between the food and the bar, talking to his business partner, Norman Wright. I recognized him from countless other gatherings.

Jeff's demeanor screamed lawyer. Nothing about his appearance stood out, he just looked like the average guy. He had dark blond hair, dark eyes, and a slender build. He also had a warm smile that beckoned us as he looked in our direction. I saved Kennedy the trouble of having to lie her way out of the place and did it for her. I turned to Norman first and then Jeff.

"Hi, Norman. Jeff, we have got to leave you all for the evening. You don't mind if I steal Kennedy away, do you? I need her expertise on some things before day's end."

"Of course, of course. You've done your time, by all means. Truth is, I'm ready for this thing to be over myself," Jeff answered.

I caught a wink from Norman who stood a wide, ridiculous grin on his face but didn't say anything. I didn't know what either gesture implied. Ignoring him, I continued.

"Please relay our farewells to Amber. We didn't want to interrupt. She's such a gracious hostess."

"Will do, Echo, will do. It's good to see you. Don't make yourself so scarce, okay?"

"I'll work on that," I said with a polite smile.

With that, we turned and departed. I couldn't wait to get away from Norman's inexplicable behavior. We had to keep ourselves from breaking into a sprint. We both let out heavy sighs as we took refuge in the seats of the convertible. The young valet—same as before— held the door as we got in, and I could swear the car looked even shinier than before. It appeared as though he'd given the car a wipe down while we were away. After sliding him a tip, Kennedy gave a wink as we took off down the driveway where the wind, once again, whipped through her hair.

Neither of us had eaten much throughout the course of the day, so we went to a restaurant near Ghiradelli Square, where Kennedy was friends with the owner and the head chef. She never had issues getting a table, no matter how many reservations were ahead of the one she *didn't* have. She'd returned to her chatty self since the awkwardness she'd felt all day had been discarded the moment we made our getaway. We compared notes of networking and strategies of reeling in potential clients. While she rambled on about a recent job she'd finished, I allowed my mind to wander, yet again. Kennedy didn't realize she'd told me this story twice already. My eyes glazed over as I wondered what I would do tomorrow.

Kennedy and Bryant often went golfing on Sundays. Skylar and Bryant had been rivals on the golf course and Kennedy had become quite good, to all of our surprise. Who knew what made her good, pride or skill, because it wasn't practice. She just refused to be outshone. I had not the hand-eye coordination for such a game; besides, it bored me. I used to go along as a spectator, to watch in amusement as the three of them carried on like children. We spent a lot of time together, the four of us but I couldn't bear to go anymore.

Something just seemed wrong about it. I didn't belong there without Skylar. So many things seemed wrong without him. I had resumed living within a brand of imposed normalcy, at least on the outside. Everyone thought I was back to "normal." What the hell is normal anyway? Why is fitting into that bracket so important? Above all else, how could I ever go from a happily married, mother-to-be to grieving widow and childless mother and ever expect to be the same person I once was? How was I to resume life in a role I'd never held nor wanted?

The waiter set a plate in front of me with a soft thunk. A plate full of something I could not recall ordering, my thoughts trapped beneath it. I flashed him a polite smile and focused on Kennedy, as she wrapped up her story. I had my response prepared and memorized. I shifted my food from one side of the plate to the other as Kennedy and I prattled on about insignificant topics, grateful to talk about things that bore no weight. It almost felt like pleasure. I ordered dessert, which was all I'd been interested in anyway. Kennedy ordered dessert wine. By the time we'd finished, the sun had set and I appreciated the darkness. We rode home, putting the top up against the chilled night air.

Kennedy asked if I would join them tomorrow, even though she knew the answer to the question. The lot of us almost never worked on Sundays. Choosing instead, to enjoy one another's company. Bryant and Skylar had become fast and good friends through no cognitive choice of their own. Kennedy and I had forced each to be in the other's wedding. Skylar and I had a large traditional wedding, though I could've done without all the frills and lace, but he'd come from an old-fashioned family. His parents, after forty-five years, were still married. Neither Skylar nor I had any siblings, so between both sets of parents they handled just about every expense for our San Francisco wedding. About a month later, we held a second reception in Boston for all those who couldn't attend, complete with slideshow of the ceremony. The massive wedding and the receptions showcased how many people knew and loved Skylar. I couldn't have been happier that of all the women in attendance, I got to be the one at the altar. I'd been given the privilege to marry him, to love him. He was more than honorable; he exhibited generosity and showed a pure love for people and those people showed up for him.

When he'd finished his internship and began a

paying position as a Physical Therapist, he made sure his parents lacked nothing. It amazed me how, at the same time, he made certain I didn't either. He'd chosen to become a nurse before striving towards Physical Therapy in order to have substantial income, allowing us to live pretty well while still in school. Although it may seem cheesy, Kennedy and I had married in the same year. We hadn't planned to nor had we dreamed of having our weddings so close together as children. It just happened that way. I married Skylar in the spring and she married Bryant in the winter. Unlike me, Kennedy couldn't wait to board the 'all eyes on me' train, floundering in the shower of attention.

Every year, the four of us vacationed together somewhere between anniversaries, kind of like a pre-celebration. One year we went to Ontario, Canada. Another year, we went to Cabo San Lucas, Mexico. The last year… the last year Skylar was alive, we went to Jamaica. Montego Bay. It's the time I dreamt of most often. The day of the week seemed to be the determining factor of whether these were dreams or nightmares.

We stayed there, in the wondrous paradise, for a week. We visited tourist attractions and local favorites. Our visit to the rum factory turned out to be quite comical. Given a drink upon entrance made the three musketeers quite happy. The smell alone seemed enough to get me tipsy. Besides, someone needed to be sober to document their drunken antics. We also went to Rick's Café to watch the cliff divers, but hadn't the courage to try. We did, however, go skinny dipping in the cave the divers jumped into. We had made a sport of playing chicken and the game never ended. Each always daring the other. None of us liked losing, no one less than Kennedy. That said, more often than not, we all participated. Bragging rights were much to valuable not to. The crowd above cheered us on, fueling our juvenile behavior. On the final day of the trip, we relaxed, laying on the beach having easy conversations. If you watched us, we behaved as if we'd been friends our entire lives. Most of our stories started with "Remember when..." In my dream, the scene played out the same as it had in real life at the moment I'd checked out of our conversational banter.

Laying out on that lounge chair, in the arms of my husband, I daydreamed about my everyday life surrounded with love, by the people who surrounded me. Not that I'd wanted to, but I couldn't imagine my life without such love, without them, without the life we'd created. I'd been blessed with an unobstructed, undiluted brand of happiness. I thought of the veil of misery my life would be, devoid of the moments we'd shared. I heard their voices but they sounded distant, like whispers of children *trying* to whisper. Someone told a joke that had been told a hundred times before.

"...because it means something different when you say it twice. Not for real...but for real, for real," they chimed in unison.

Cradled within the folds of Skylar's limbs, I felt him laugh beneath me. Leaning against his chest, I charted the path of his laugh from his basement of his belly, through his diaphragm and out of his mouth. The baritone of his infectious laugh danced around my ears. How the same joke still made laugh, I'll never know, but I giggled in the midst of my other thoughts. My trance continued, as did the banter. Moments later, I felt Skylar's laughter trembling beneath me again. He seemed like a dream to me sometimes, but instead of pinching myself to make sure I existed, I'd rather touch him to make certain that he did.

The Jamaican sun had altered our textures. I'd developed a fascination with the contrast in our skin tones. He had become a caramelized hue of honey and I had been dusted with copper, although my skin usually resembled a shade of cypress wood. I found beauty in the mixture between his skin and mine. With my fingertips, I traced the length of his arm, following with my eyes. He never seemed to notice when I traced him or maybe he had just grown accustomed to it. In secret, I think he enjoyed these gestures that appeared to be absent of mind. He laced his fingers into mine and rested them atop my abdomen, but not before planting a kiss on my palm. I'd smiled as I scanned our bodies and then stared into the ocean. The call of my name brought me back into the conversation they'd been having and I rejoined the colloquy. I'd lifted my arms up behind me and wrapped them around Skylar's neck trying to get closer to him, if that were even possible.

"We're home, honey," Kennedy sang, as if on cue.

She chimed in at the same moment I'd always waken. Kennedy and I were sitting in front of my building. Through the glass doors, I saw Gary sitting behind the wide, circular island in the middle of the lobby. He glanced up for a moment and gave a curt wave, then he went back to watching the monitors situated inside the large piece of furniture. I wondered if he had a personal television back there to watch things a little more entertaining than empty hallways and a motionless parking lots. I turned to Kennedy, feeling guilty, as though I'd ignored her all day.

"Thanks, love," I began. "I hope I wasn't a total bore for you today."

"Are you kidding me! Anything would've been better than going alone—except maybe for bringing Bryant, of course. He would have, no doubt, made it worse. He would have left me to deal with Amber alone. He knows how I get in that kind of situation. I can't imagine how this day would have gone without you. I might have insulted the poor woman, not on purpose, of course. How are you, dear? You did very well, minus that awkward belly stare you gave her." She chuckled.

"I know. God, I can't believe I froze up like that. Thanks for the help by the way." I jabbed my elbow into her side.

"What was I supposed to do? Hell, I didn't know what to say! I just tried to keep from touching her. I hear morning sickness is a mess—a big one!"

We both laughed, but I think for different reasons. I laughed at her, whether she knew that or not, but I'm sure she did. A low ringing interrupted our animated smiles. We both sifted around for our phones but I wasn't surprised that hers had been the one ringing.

"It's Bryant." She peeked at the caller ID. "The husband beckons. Probably wants to know if I'll be home for dinner; it's his turn to cook. Maybe I should tell him I've already eaten, or should I just be polite and eat again?"

"It's always his turn to cook and since when have you been polite?" I laughed.

She didn't answer the phone. Instead, we bid farewell with promises to call the next day. As I waved at her from inside, I saw her putting her earpiece in place, no doubt to return Bryant's phone call. I checked the mail on the way upstairs. The box overflowed, lots of which looked like junk mail. I couldn't remember the last time I'd checked the mail. It didn't feel like too long ago, at least not long enough to amass such a heap. I had to use both hands to carry it all. Trying to retrieve my keys caused half of it to spill to the floor. I almost left it there for building maintenance to clean up.

Once inside the condo, I littered the kitchen counter with the papers and headed to our room. I undressed, putting everything in its place and took another shower, taking pause to enjoy it. I washed my hair and stood under the spray until my skin turned fevered and red. Wrapping my hair and body in separate towels, I air dried while putting a kettle on for tea. While the tea steeped, I donned one of Skylar's old college shirts from Northeastern University. Despite my zaftig figure, his shirt swallowed me. Lost within it made me feel as if his arms were around me once again. I folded myself into one of the two chairs in the living room and sipped my mint tea, while staring at the dark waters of the San Francisco Bay.

I didn't bother turning on the television, for I knew I wouldn't watch it but I did know that I'd dream of him when I went to sleep, just as I had every night since the accident. As I slipped under the covers of our bed, feeling the coolness against my exposed flesh, I wondered. I wondered how long my life would revolve in the same pattern. The pattern of living as if he wasn't dead, of dreaming of moments passed, never to be lived again; of queries of what our baby would have been like, who would he favor, what would we have named her. I wondered how long I would torture myself with questions I couldn't answer.

I wanted to get to a place where I could smile at the fond memories of him, in spite of all that I'd lost. I wanted to find happiness in the life we'd shared without the sorrow overshadowing it. I wanted to move forward, but fear of living as if he wasn't with me kept me tethered to the past. Fear also kept me from feeling the reality of being alone. Releasing the fear would mean acceptance. Acceptance meant moving beyond denial. Could I be ready for that?

While I wasn't in denial that he was gone, I was in denial that I would have to live a life free of him, of his things, of memories. I still wore my wedding ring and slept pushed to the edge of the bed because he always slept so close to me. I still had his cell phone on my speed dial, and every so often, I'd call it, hoping he'd answer. Our answering machine still had his recoded greeting, the one medium for which I could ever hear his voice again. I kept the house in the order he insisted on, even now, trying not to disappoint him. How could I live as if he didn't exist, when he still felt present to me?

Where would I find joy, happiness, glee? Where would I find right when everything seems all wrong? Where would I find the courage, the manual, not to move on, but to move? If I could just move in any direction, it would be progress. I'd been stuck in a time warp for close to eighteen months. I lived in constant wait for him to reappear, to come home from work, to wake me with gentle kisses upon my back, the way he often did. I just want to be able to move. Questions continued to roll nonstop as slumber found refuge upon my eyelids. My mind would not rest. It kept asking question after question but no answers came.

Two

With a gentle touch, he swept my hair aside, his fingertips grazing my neck. A pleasant shudder of electricity coursed through me. Though I couldn't see him, I knew his touch, his pattern of breathing. His energy awakened my nerves, making them apparent, undeniable. Everywhere they touched, his soft lips ignited sparks. Miniature fires lit along my neck and the length of my spine with each of his kisses. I squirmed, a sinful smile trekked across my lips while a rising heat enveloped me. Had summer come already? The sun shone through the windows with the first light of morning. In the meantime, the fires Skylar had kindled grew, intensifying with every touch.

"Beautiful morning, Sky…" My voice sounded a little raspy but his response remained the same.

"Dreaming of love's Echo."

It had become our standard morning greeting, a simple play on names, spiked with love. Although the words were a part of our everyday, it didn't make them any less true or meaningful. Skylar was beautiful to me. His beauty shone like daybreak. Magnificent to everyone who'd gaze upon the morning Sky. He was my sunrise. My Beautiful Morning Sky. With unabashed sincerity, he often told me of how he'd dreamt of a love that mimicked his, for a heart that would beat in unison, to spout sonnets of Love and have them return with as much fervor for which he'd expelled them. His Love's Echo.

I rolled over to face him, eager to feel his brand of sunshine on my face and he did not disappoint. His radiant smile and sparkling eyes danced shadows over my face. We needed no words, our expressions said more than vowels and syllables. He leaned close enough for me to smell his faded cologne and closer still to kiss my lips. As he closed the minuscule distance between us, I felt heat emanating from him. The temperature rose a few degrees with every disappearing inch. His lips were a whisper away, and I moved closer to fuse the gap—knock!

"Oww!" I heard someone say.

The voice sounded close to my ears. I pried my eyes open, realizing the voice I'd heard belonged to me as did the headache. I'd migrated to Skylar's side of the bed and had, therefore, knocked my head on his nightstand. *Some kiss!* Why couldn't my dreams include the good parts?

Instead, I always woke before I got close enough to really feel him. Should I classify that as a nightmare, then? To me, it felt like it. I sat up in bed, pulling the sheets over my torso. Well, at least I didn't cry in my sleep anymore. I'd substituted that for sweaty nights.

I got up and stripped the bed, tossing the comforter and sheets to the floor. Seeing them there, gave me a childlike urge to run and fall into them, roll around and wrap myself up like a burrito. So I did. I laughed, and somewhere in my imagination, I heard Skylar laugh too. I lay there amid the rumpled linens, limbs and hair spread out in every direction, catching my breath. I felt strange. Not as though I were losing my mind, but in some weird way, finding it.

A sudden vigor infused me. I hopped up too fast, and my head swam. Once the room stopped spinning, I gathered the sheets from the floor and put them in the wash, recovering the bed and pillows with fresh, crisp sheets. I took a cool shower to lower my body temperature and extinguish the tiny fires my dream had started. Even in the afterlife, that man could stir me. A feeling of spontaneity washed over me like lather, and I decided to take a drive to Santa Cruz. Although, being in cars still made me nervous and, if I'm being honest, a little paranoid, but not as much if drove myself. The drive would just take an hour and a half. I could handle that. Besides, I had a bit of incentive. Santa Cruz had a quaint bookstore that I'd become fond of. Yes, that is what I'll do and I needed to enjoy the time because the workload for the next day would be heavy because of several events.

It seemed all the questions last night had given me some resolve. The many questions I'd never asked myself, because I wasn't ready to answer them and didn't think I could. Could this be a roundabout affirmation that I was ready to move? Had my subconscious given me a push? Though my mind still brimmed with questions, my spirit had taken a step. A small step. In which direction, I did not know, nor did I care. I'd moved!

Excited, I moved around the room, energized. Pulling out my beach bag, I crammed it full of things I needed and some I didn't. I slipped on my swimsuit and then put on a pair of white shorts and flouncy, yellow top. Then, I pulled half my hair up into a ponytail, grabbed a pair of sandals, and headed into the kitchen. I opened the refrigerator and stood there staring at the carton of milk, but didn't reach for it, realizing, in that moment, that the need no longer existed. I had no baby and no escalating hormones to make my stomach churn with nausea, a remedy for a problem I no longer had. Letting the refrigerator door close, I turned around to the scattered mail splayed on the counter. Even though I wasn't in the mood, I felt obligated to, at least, sift through it.

"Bill, bill, crap, bill, junk." I tossed each envelope aside.

It all looked the same, except one…two. One came as an official letter from a bank I didn't recognize as one Skylar or I had used. Skylar's name had been printed on the front along with his office address. Adhered below, a yellow sticker indicated a forwarding address—ours. I opened the letter, wondering what could be inside. Discarding the envelope and unfolding the paper, I began reading but stopped once I recognized it as an advertisement. However, I did wonder why did it read "Dear Customer" but I blew it off as a mistake. Still, one more letter remained and my curiosity urged me to read it. The business letter had my name scrawled across the front in elegant penmanship. The handwriting was lovely, fancy even. It reminded me of calligraphy when society considered it art and you were considered talented, if you could master it. However, not like in our modern world where drawn script came from a computer generated font type.

Before I turned it over to open it, I noticed the lack of a return address, nor did it have any postage. No post markings, smudges, or ink blots—nothing. Just a crisp, white envelope sealed with tape at the back, bearing my name and address. I pulled the tape away from the stark envelope and slid out the folded paper. It held a single sheet, much too small for such a large envelope. On the sheet read one question, in large typed print: HOW MUCH DO YOU KNOW? I flipped it over making sure there wasn't something I'd missed. Blank. I didn't understand. All of a sudden I felt dyslexic, as if I'd read it wrong or backwards. So I read it twice more, but the confusion remained the same. How much do I know about what? How much should I know? How the hell am I supposed to answer the question if there's no information in which to respond? The letter made me feel angry and annoyed by the stupidity of its inquiry. I wished I'd left that stupid pile of mail right where I'd put it last night. I dropped the letter back to the counter, pushed my irritation to the pits of my mind and focused on my movements in a very literal way. I walked out of the door in less than two minutes.

In the parking lot, I dumped my packed bag and purse in the front seat of my Volvo. Sometimes I wished for the coupe instead of an SUV. The extra space sometimes made me feel a bit lonesome, but it came in handy, often fundamental, for work. It made cargo transport easy. It had been Skylar's idea to buy the XC90. The model sounded like a random jumble of letters and numbers, meaning nothing to me. Skylar had wanted to ensure my safety above all things, and I couldn't be grateful for that, given my paranoia. I felt safe in the vehicle while he continued to drive the twenty-year-old BMW convertible he'd had since college. I must say, he kept it in pristine condition. Boys and their cars. I shook my head at the thought of him polishing and buffing the aged car. My old junker had been a hazard to everything and everybody. I'd driven a persnickety Honda Civic hatchback that sputtered and backfired much too often.

I made it to the 101 south ramp quicker than I'd expected, heaven knows I hadn't been speeding. Before entering the highway, I stopped to grab a cup of coffee and a muffin from a nearby café. I merged onto the 101, checking my mirrors before merging into traffic. The lanes were clear, so I sped up but before reaching the average speed or changing lanes, a motorcycle materialized out of nowhere. It sped by, its roaring engine startling the crap out of me. I swerved right and slammed the brakes. Part of me wanted to scream at the biker for being so reckless and even more, curse him for frightening me, increasing my already paranoid state of mind, assuming the driver was a man. The biker had moved past me too fast to see much, except for one its color.

The motorcycle had been a sparkling shade of green sprinkled with glitter, each speck a glorious reflection in the sunlight. Behind me, horns blared by the hands of their impatient drivers. Despite the urgency from behind, I sat for a moment longer waiting for my mind to send signals to my body to move. What I really wanted to do was put the car in reverse, back down the ramp, park it, and walk home but something inside me wouldn't allow it. Shaking my head loose of the fear, determined to keep momentum, I inched forward, checking mirrors and blind spots time and again. Another horn blared as someone rushed around me, jarring my confidence yet again. Feeling frustrated with myself and everyone else, I moved forward at a steady pace until, at last, I'd merged into the moving traffic. I needed to calm myself because I didn't want to go home. I didn't want to be afraid of driving, or cars, or traffic, or life. I needed to live again, to smile and mean it, to enjoy...that's it, just to enjoy and not just endure. With that in mind, I put on some classical music. A little Ludwig and Frederic would relax me. The music filled the cabin and my mind went adrift, gliding into my last moments with Skylar.

We were on our way to the golf course, as usual, on a Sunday afternoon, to meet Bryant and Kennedy. Skylar had let the top down in his BMW while we drove through the streets of San Francisco having a conversation about nothing. I giggled at something he'd said, as he so often made a spectacle of himself just to make me laugh. He loved my laugh, although I found it to be quite goofy. He amused me just to coax a particular laugh out of me. We sat at a stop light and he reached over, placing his hand on my belly. The smile on his face grew, stretching wide from one side to the other, dazzling me. His eyes danced when he looked up from my stomach and into my eyes. I covered his hand with mine and I still remember thinking of how lucky I'd been to have such love; a husband, conjured by dreams and a baby destined for beauty inside and out, thanks to him. He said something I didn't hear, so I leaned a little closer, resting my head against the headrest and turning my ear towards him.

"Did you hear me when I said I love you?" he asked. I felt the quizzical expression fade from my face and replaced it with a smile.

"No, say it again." My answer never changed.

The little white lie between us had become a mischievous game we played just to hear the things our hearts couldn't get enough of. He removed his hand and progressed through the green traffic light but halted again a few yards away by another red one. Once at a stop, he turned to me and pushed a strand of hair out of my face, tracing it behind my ear and down my neck.

"I love you, Echo Wells," He leaned down to talk to my belly. "And you too, little Wells."

I giggled, finding it a little absurd and a lot adorable.

"Sky," I said through my smile, my hand rubbing his back as he hunched over my lap. "Green light."

He sat up, showing no urgency whatsoever, and gave the green light a glimpse before ambling forward. We were still smiling when…

Damn! I missed my exit to highway 17. I'd have to double back which I hated doing. Between the music and my thoughts, I'd lost myself in a labyrinth so I navigated my way back to the highway I'd missed, trying to figure out how I had made it onto the one before that.

It wasn't long before I arrived in Santa Cruz. The bookstore I loved sat right in the hub of the city, on a corner, amid other shops with storefronts shaded with bright colors. Most of them boasted extravagant window dressings with sale signs, meant to lure the prospective customer inside. The bookstore, dubbed *Pages of Phrases*, still showcased its original paint color, save for the front door. A deep mahogany brown colored the frame. The two columns that didn't appear to hold up any part of the structure had been painted with a lighter shade of brown.

The ocean blue door stood out as the single, most obvious variation. I felt a lopsided smile lift my cheeks the moment I alighted from my truck. Walking up to the door, I noticed the one sign in their window read OPEN. Simple, I like it. I stepped inside and the old-fashioned bell clanged above the doorjamb.

"Hello there!" An exuberant man's voice came from somewhere behind a stack of books.

My crooked smile transformed into a full-fledged grin, pulling at the muscles of my face. I felt it spread from one side to the other, and what do you know, it was real. For the first time in a long time I'd smiled and meant it.

"Hi!" I sang, even though, I had not spotted the person who'd spoken.

I peered around shelves, looking towards the register, which sat in an odd space at the farthest, corner of the store but saw no one.

"Is there anything I can help you find, dear?"

"Uh, n—no. I'll just find my way around. I'll send out a search party if I need anything."

"Very well, then," he said, giving a little laugh.

I'd almost forgotten how much I loved the store. An older British couple, Harold and Jeanne Kenier, owned it. Despite their many years in the states, they'd never misplaced their accents. They had been married for quite a number of years. When no one watched, they behaved like teenagers in love, making me wonder if I'd ever feel that way again, about someone other than Skylar that is.

Being a true lover of the written word, *Pages of Phrases* brought me instant joy. Books crammed every empty space in the store. Books were stacked on shelves and above, from top to bottom. They lined the walls and crowded the floors. The hardest thing wasn't finding a good or worthy book, but figuring out where to start looking for one. They had everything from Shakespeare to comics, travel to picture books, novels to biographies—a literary oasis. Books with worn covers and aged yellow pages weren't in short supply either. It seemed dust and age were prerequisites for any book to occupy the shelves. I loved that most, maybe even all, of the books came from people and not other stores or manufacturers. You'd often find handwritten inscriptions inside the covers, personal notes to a loved one, a stamp of history. It reminded of a passport, each stamp telling of where the book had traveled and to whom it once belonged.

Browsing the aisles in awe, I read nothing, but touched everything, taking in the smell of matured words and stories. At some point, I got around to picking something, but it seemed a cruel fate, like choosing a favorite child over his brothers. So I selected five. Three weathered books: one of which bore the inscription: to 'My Lily in the valley, my flower among weeds, my love of all loves. Love, Dad' dated March 8, 1972. The others were somewhat "new."

Harold rang me up at a snail's pace using an antique

cash register with long, raised keys oversized display window. Despite the modern advances in technology and his wife still kept a hand written sales log. He wrote my purchases in his ledger making shaky, deliberate strokes with his pen.

"Thanks, Harold. See you next time!" I smiled again.

"Make it soon, yeah?"

"I'll try."

As usual, time had escaped me, lost in the presence of books and words. My growling stomach reminded me that needed to eat. I had planned to have lunch on the wharf anyway, just not so late in the afternoon. However, it felt good not to count every hour or every minute as it ticked by. Contentment enveloped me and I reveled in the beauty of being wrapped in an emotion other than misery or even nostalgia.

I scouted the wharf for the least crowded restaurant possible and seated myself in a corner booth, pulled out a book and began to read. There weren't many people in the restaurant so I didn't look up much except when the waiter came by and when I paused to gaze out the window. The tall windows faced the open water, where ships passed. I watched them sail by, a welcome change from my normal people-watching. Instead, I got lost in the never-ending swell of the sea.

"Excuse me, Miss. Is everything okay here?"

I looked up.

"Oh, yes. I'm sorry. I'm just a little lost in my book here." I gestured to the book in my hand.

A man dressed in a pair of pressed slacks, dress shirt and tie stood next to my table. He had a pleasant-looking smile with tiny crow's feet clawing at the corner of each blue eye. The sun had streaked his light blond hair, cut close on the sides and spiky on top. It looked as if he'd smiled again, even though the first smile never left his face.

"Ah, I see. I was a little reluctant to disturb you, but I noticed you haven't touched your meal. I just wanted to ensure that you were satisfied with everything."

Looking down at my plate, I realized what he meant. I hadn't eaten much, at all, maybe a bite or two, neither of which I remembered. Where had my hunger gone? I'd been feasting on words and had neglected to feed my body. My stomach made an audible growl. My cheeks flushed with embarrassment, making the stranger laugh. I searched my mind for something to say, sifting through words which made no sense for the situation. He saved me from drowning myself.

"I won't insult you by offering to heat that, but it seems you're still hungry. I could have the chef prepare you a fresh entrée, if you'd like, at no charge of course." He paused. "By the way, I'm Seth. Seth Nelson." He held his hand out to me and reached out to shake it. "I own this place...and you are?"

"Echo. Echo Wells."

"Very nice to meet you, Miss Wells." He emphasized the Miss, making it sound like Mizz.

Maybe he didn't see the wedding ring on my finger. I felt for the ring with the pad of my thumb to twirl it around my finger the way I assumed everyone did. My eyes grew wide as my thumb felt the warmth of skin instead of the cool, precious metal I'd expected. Struggling to keep my face passive and restrain the building panic, I tried to concentrate on answering his question. What had he ask me again? Something about food...perhaps. I couldn't remember and gave up.

"Forgive me," I said. "What did you ask me again?"

The owner had been gracious enough to repeat his question—offering again to make a new entrée for me and adding that reheated seafood wouldn't taste as great. I declined the offer, asking for a take-out box, instead.

"Let me, at least, get you some dessert since you're insulting me by not eating my food and refusing to let me make it better."

How had his smile gotten larger? It didn't seem possible but he'd begun to speak my language. My eyes must have brightened at the mention of dessert because his body appeared to relax. I couldn't quite describe how, but I'd seen the tiny change. He took my brightening eyes as a sign of acceptance—smart move—and began listing the desserts they offered, including one of his favorites: a mixed berry tart with homemade raspberry gelato. I wasn't a fan of gelato, so I didn't choose his favorite, but requested a dessert with real ice cream. Before leaving my table, he left a comment card for me to fill out.

"It's the least you can do." We both chuckled.

As soon as he disappeared from sight, I began searching for my ring, frantic at the thought of losing it. I checked my finger first, as if my eyes would make it appear or as though my thumb had been wrong in its feeling. I searched the table, floor, my purse, my bag, and my pockets—nothing! Where is it? Tears smarted my eyes, blurring my vision and my breathing grew rapid. Making my way through a maze of dinner tables, I rushed to the bathroom, making it before my tears broke the dam, but not by much. Leaning over the sink, laboring to breathe, I stared at my naked finger.

"Calm down and think," I said aloud.

My face flushed with heat, blotching my skin red. I washed my hands and splashed cold water on my face. Then, a little light bulb came on above my head.

When Skylar and I first got engaged, and then married, I refused to take off my rings for anything, not a bath, not a shower, nothing. Because of that, Skylar would often take them to get cleaned. Lotions and moisturizers congealed on and between the diamonds. Once, my ring had almost tumbled down the drain...okay, twice. My soapy hands had caused it to slip off and into the sink...and the shower.

Thinking on those things, I remembered removing it earlier to lave my body with sun block, being as how I had planned to lie out on the beach—something I still had not done. In my newfound excitement, I had left it on the vanity. I saw it in my mind's eye and exhaled a long, shaky sigh of relief. Could this be a sign?

In one week, it would mark a year and a half since I'd lost Skylar, since I'd lost our baby, since the demise of our family. How far along should I be in my recovery from grief? Is there a time line to follow? I didn't think myself ready for as much progress as not wearing my wedding ring implied, but for the moment, I had no choice.

Calm enough to rejoin society, I went back to my table and I saw the owner making his way there as well. *What's his name again? Had I even listened when he introduced himself?* I sat down before he reached my table but I still couldn't recall his name. He sat the dessert in front of me and gathered my plates full of cold food. I thought he would box it right there, but he sat down another box and took the plates away.

"Enjoy, Mizz Wells. Be sure to come back and visit us." His never fading smile didn't waver.

Before I could protest about him taking away my meal, he'd moved to another table halfway across the room. I watched in disbelief as he handed my plates off to a waiter passing by, before he greeted the patrons at the next table.

Why did he do that? Why would he bring me an empty box and take my food away? I jabbed the cardboard box with a disgruntled finger, but it didn't move. I pulled the unexpected weight towards me and before I could open it, I felt the heat of the box and smelled the food inside. I opened it and saw a spread of steaming seafood placed as though it were art instead of food. It made me hungry all over again, but I refused to let the dessert go to waste.

Not long after I'd finished my scrumptious dessert, my waiter appeared. He cleared the dishes and left the bill at the edge of the table. I took a moment to fill out the comment card the owner had left and placed it into the little leather binder. Looking at the charges on the paper inside, I noticed meal had been listed by item, including the complimentary dessert, but the total came to zero dollars and two cents. *Was this a joke?*

I looked around and caught a vision of the sun, inching to hid behind the sea. Once I had all my belongings together, I summoned the waiter, asking him to explain the bill. He didn't say much except to reveal that the rest had been taken care of. It wasn't much of an explanation.

"Is the owner still here?" I asked, still unable to recall his name.

"No, I'm afraid he's gone for the evening."

You've got to be kidding me. I didn't know what to make of it, so I tipped the waiter, paid my two cent bill and left. I smiled as I walked the wharf, stopping at a jewelry store along the way. A necklace in the window caught my eye. It had the same patterned links as my anklet, a perfect match. I browsed the store while making up my mind about whether to buy the necklace. In the end, I voted yes. I couldn't think back far enough to when I'd bought something I'd wanted.

By the time I finished shopping, the sun had set. I needed to get back to the city, my city but I took a casual stroll back to my truck anyway. Once inside, I decided to listen to some music to complement my mood. Rock, seemed the apt fit. I sang aloud to the album from one of my favorite bands, *The Fray*, and bopped my head to their music the entire way home. The drive flew by, feeling like half an hour rather than an hour and a half. At home, I pulled into my designated parking spot, turned off the engine and gathered my bag and the things I'd acquired in Santa Cruz. While I consolidated bags I heard a thump or, at least, I thought I'd heard a noise. With a start, I looked around at every car in sight to see if anyone lingered inside their vehicles. No one. I hadn't seen anyone else in the parking lot. I checked for movement through my rearview mirror. At first, I didn't see anything, making me feel paranoid, then I saw dark figure walk by. I whipped around but, again, no one. In the next instant, the figure appeared at my passenger window. A short yelp escaped my mouth, followed by a quick rap on the window. Putting his hands up in surrender, the man took a step back from my window.

"Geez, Gary! You scared the crap out of me!" I said

on a fraction of breath and let out a relieved sigh.

Gary, the security guard, pulled the door open for me.

"I didn't mean to scare you, Mrs. Wells." An apologetic expression contorted his aging features. "My apologies. Just checking to see if you needed any help upstairs."

He opened the back door and grabbed my other shopping bag. I'd always liked Gary, with his deep southern accent and old-school southern charm, ever the gentleman. Although, I wondered how secure I should feel with him standing guard. From short conversations I'd had with him, I knew he'd served in the Army, but his age remained a mystery to me. His graying hair and creamy skin, gave way to wrinkles in some places while leaving others untouched. He walked as though he were seven feet tall and with the gait of a much younger man. On another deep breath, I thanked Gary for helping me. He carried my bags and escorted me to my door. He had been going an extra few miles to look after me since I could remember, often telling me I reminded him of his daughter, whom he missed so much.

"Goodnight, Mrs. Wells." He smiled. "So sorry again for that scare I gave you."

"Goodnight, Gary. Thanks for your help."

"My pleasure." He turned on his heel and strode away.

I smiled after him as he walked down the hall, exuding confidence and commanding attention. I imagined the catch he must have been in his younger years; he still seemed one now.

Unlocking the door, I went inside and placed my bags on top of the disordered mail from the day before and ran straight for the bathroom. Right where I thought it would be lay my wedding band. I put it back in its rightful place and stared at it, shifting it with one finger and then the next. On a sigh, I returned to the living room to put away my things. When I pulled the take-out from out of the bag it made me hungry again, after all, I'd eaten nothing but dessert, even if it had been a good one. I almost popped it in the microwave but then I thought of how insulted the restaurant owner would be if he knew I'd reheated the food that way and "ruined the texture of the dish" as he'd put it. I couldn't remember the guy's name, but his cooking tips, that I remembered, so I steamed my dish, instead.

While food warmed on the stove, I put my books away. When Skylar and I first moved in, we had the second bedroom set up as an office and library. Skylar changed that almost the instant he found out we were going to have a baby. He and Bryant moved the massive bookshelves into the living area, resting each against one of the few solid walls in the house and placed our desk next to the front door. At first, I thought it was an unusual and illogical place to put a desk, but it proved quite convenient. Aside from that, it occupied the vacant, white space before the wall of windows, offering a wonderful view from that seat.

On the shelf, I found empty spaces for the books I'd bought, adding them to my growing collection. Skylar's eyes caught mine from a picture of the two of us framed there. I still remembered the moment. We had taken a weekend trip to Miami, Florida. Since both of us had grown up in wintry states, we took full advantage of the sun and all its glory. We loved the heat, and when paired with the beach, it always felt like the perfect vacation. We'd stayed at a hotel right on the strip in South Beach, having lazy mornings in bed and opting for breakfast delivered by room service in lieu of a bustling restaurant. We'd eaten on the balcony overlooking the beach, kicking our feet up on the rail while immersed in conversation and easy laughter. We didn't leave our room until the latter part of the afternoon.

We'd walked the beach, enjoying the water as it lapped at our feet. It felt as if we'd walked for miles, our steps untraceable, as the water erased all signs of our journey. Skylar had snapped pictures of us, stretching his long arms out in front of us to get the shot. In every frame, our faces had filled the lens. It left almost no room for scenery, forcing him to take those pictures without us in them. When I'd try to snap a photo of us, both faces wouldn't even find the lens, leaving fractions of us unseen.

A passerby offered to take a picture of the two of us together. Skylar stood almost an entire foot above me. Most times, his chin had found rest on the crown of my head. At one time, it annoyed me, but like most other things about Skylar, he transformed the annoying into charming, sometimes comical. The guy who took the picture chuckled as he snapped. Skylar had draped his arms in an "X" across my chest and I'd held on to him. We'd thanked the stranger and looked at the display on the screen. I looked almost childlike alongside his brawny figure. We both chuckled at the picture And Skylar returned to snapping our candid close ups. He'd said something amusing just before taking the next shot, which made our smiles even bigger. I couldn't decide which picture I liked best, so they shared a single space between lines of books.

My eyes filled with tears, distorting the images before me. I swiped at them with the back of my hand and stood there, entranced by the photos for a time, until the phone rang. The sound filled the condo and as I looked at the phone on the desk, I realized that I hadn't seen or heard my cell phone all day. I didn't even know I'd brought it with me. I made a mental note to look for it and then reached for the home phone. I cleared my throat, hoping it would excise any audible signals of distress. I couldn't be sure of how many times the phone had rung but if I didn't answer soon, Skylar's voice would be the next sound in the room and that would pierce my already bleeding heart.

As ancient as it may seem, in our home of modern and advanced technologies, Skylar had insisted on using a physical answering machine rather than voicemail. Something nostalgic about it appealed to him. He liked staying tethered to certain simplicities. I hadn't the right to say much about it, considering I had a bookshelf full of thirty and forty-year-old books. As a gift for my birthday, someone had given me an electronic book reader and until this day, it remained boxed and unopened, sharing space with the audio books given to me by another someone. Skylar knew better than to touch that trademark of mine. I refused to give up the touch, feel, and smell, of actual books, so I didn't fight him on the answering machine.

"Hello," I answered, working to keep my voice even.

"Hi, sweetie. Where've you been? I've been trying to get ahold of you all day. Why didn't you answer the phone? I've been worried. I swear if you didn't answer the phone just now, I would've been over there. Are you okay? What are you doing and why do you sound so tense?"

"Hi, Kennedy." My voice sounded drab. "I'm sorry. I didn't mean to worry you. I drove to Santa Cruz today and I haven't been home long."

"You could've just answered the phone to tell me that, you know. You didn't have to ignore me. Why didn't you tell me? How did it go—the drive, I mean?"

"I wasn't ignoring you, Kennedy. I don't even know where my cell phone is. I have to find it. I visited that mom and pop bookstore I like so much and got lost." I smiled at the thought. "I wound up spending the entire day there and having lunch on the wharf—oh, geez!"

I dropped the phone and ran into the kitchen. I heard the receiver as it clattered onto the desk while I raced to turn off the fire under the pot of my warming food. The water had almost boiled away, but a tiny puddle remained but the rest of the dry places had begun to scorch. I dashed back to the phone hoping Kennedy hadn't had a coronary.

"Echo! What the hell is going on! What—"

"Sorry, I forgot I had food on the stove. I needed to catch it before I burned down the building," I interrupted. "I'm okay, Kennedy, I swear. Stop worrying so much. I just want to sit down and eat now. I'll give you a buzz tomorrow; we can have lunch."

She agreed, though she sounded reluctant, and we hung up. *How long had I been standing there staring at that picture?* My meal would've been ruined, perhaps, burned if I hadn't steamed it. Relieved, I plated my food, curled up on one end of the couch and grabbed the remote. I clicked through channels until I found something I could watch without having to pay much attention to it. I looked over at the picture on the shelf once more, but the aroma wafting from my plate pulled my attention. Ravenous, I devoured the delicious meal in mere minutes, cleaning up after myself and sorting the mail afterwards. Making a neat pile of bills that needed paying on the desk and discarding the junk mail, again, I came across the anonymous letter but wasn't sure what to do with it. So, I put it into the desk drawer. I didn't have the wherewithal to think on it any further. Thinking of the full week ahead, I turned off the television and climbed into bed.

Three

The weeks had flown by, like rapid winds carrying with it spores of new life. Kennedy and I had made some fruitful new business connections and the avalanche of projects and parties had us in a constant tumble. It seemed she and I had collaborated more in the past few months than in our entire careers. Working with her made my job much more fun than I'd ever imagined, she made it impossible not to enjoy myself. Our clients seemed to feel the same.

In addition to my "playdates" with Kennedy, I received a bouquet of flowers at least once a week, accompanied by an unsigned card. The delivery service had no more information than I did, so they said. Sometimes, I'd receive a treat as well, some kind of sweet. After a while, I'd stopped trying to figure out who might be sending the generous gifts. I'd acquired so many new clients that even speculation would take too much time to pinpoint. In any case, this person would, I hoped, tire of anonymity and reveal themselves.

Given my state of industriousness, I hadn't much trouble sleeping anymore. By the end of the day, my body was so worn out, sometimes I couldn't even muster enough energy to shower. Some days I didn't crawl into bed until the next morning. In fact, that seemed to be most days. My schedule had been flooded with events, dinners, lunches, and drink meetings, often following me into unconsciousness. I'd started to keep a notepad and pen on the nightstand to write down ideas that came to me in the night. I still dreamt of Skylar, but not every night as I once had. Most nights, I'd still adhere to my side of the bed. Missing him and loving him, though an inseparable part of me, didn't feel as painful. Part of me felt guilty, yet another, sad and afraid, as if moving on would, somehow, betray his memory.

Skylar and I had talked about our lives and what we'd dreamed for our individual selves and each other. We'd also talked about death and what we'd hoped for the other, should one of us be left alive. At the time, once seemed too many and I could not imagine a life without him. It's not something I wanted to think of, much less discuss, regardless of how necessary it might have been. Many couples leave discussion for "later" and when later becomes now, they're left perplexed in the wake of the unfortunate death of a loved one, never having known what they would've wanted for themselves or the widowed. If I didn't know any better, I would have thought Skylar had peeked into the future and prepared me for it. Not that I could have ever *prepared* to lose such a significant love or my child who would have been a beautiful representative treasure of Skylar. There's no class, no discussion big enough, long enough, or thorough enough for a tragedy so great.

Skylar had told me about the life he wanted for our child and me. Of course, like a good husband, he wanted me to be happy, no matter what, with or without him. He'd been so excited to become a father and I'm relieved he didn't know we'd lost our baby. I found a small margin of solace in the fact that he hadn't suffered the pain of losing our child. I wondered if he'd realized how big a role he'd played in my happiness? He couldn't have known, because if he had, he would have also known how ridiculous it sounded to not have happiness and him in the same space. Happiness without him...could there be such a thing?

Regardless of how I felt about it, I thought of what he wanted for me and that had helped me to move forward. I never wanted to disappoint him, for he had never disappointed me. He may have annoyed me, angered me, or irritated me but not once had he disappointed me.

With all the new clientele, I'd forced myself to take a step forward, even though I didn't feel ready. What choice did I have? Clients asked inevitable questions about my life, after all, I'd been privy to theirs. They wondered about my history, my leisure time. Bryant, on occasion, had joined

Kennedy at one event or the other, giving clients a glimpse into her personal life, making them all the more curious about mine. They connected with her in a way they hadn't with me. So came the comments—some less innocent than others:"Your husband is one lucky guy". "Apologize to your husband for me, I know we've been taking up a lot of your time".

One client had asked when they'd get to meet my "mysterious husband". I'd avoid each of their questions as best I could, dodging their subtle hints and rejecting invitations, but how long could that go on? It hurt to think of the answer to every query or the retort to each comment. Some nights, I cried because I hated the responses, almost as much as I hated the reality. I couldn't deny how the course of events had forced me into acceptance. The questions, however, I could respond to any way I wanted. I could conjure Skylar up and make him live and breathe again through my words. He would be an almost tangible love but the hardest part about conjuring him up was returning home and discovering he wasn't there waiting for me as I'd said. I couldn't stand to lose him again, even if it only happened in my head, so I took one hesitant, but drastic step forward: I took off my wedding ring.

The sense of emptiness made me cry. While staring at my jewelry box with wet eyes, I noticed an unopened box. I opened it as though it were a gift. Inside, I found the necklace I'd bought three months ago in Santa Cruz, having forgotten all about it. The timing could not have been more perfect. In lieu of confining my ring to a box in my closet, I threaded the necklace through the ring and wore it around my neck. I felt a lot less like I'd abandoned Skylar although it took some getting used to. I wasn't quite there yet.

Tonight would be another late one. Kennedy and I had a large event to ready ourselves for, beginning this afternoon. I woke up not long after sunrise, determined to get a jump-start on the day and give myself a few minutes to breathe before the melée began. Still in my pajamas, I walked down to check the mail. Gary's smiling face greeted me in the lobby.

"Good morning, Mrs. Wells." His tone rang with enthusiasm. He had such a refreshing personality.

"Good morning, Gary. How are you?"

"I can't complain." He shook his head.

I pulled the few pieces of mail from the box, grateful it wasn't an arm load. I spotted a few bills, which I had expected, and the usual junk mail.

"There's another special delivery for you here, Mrs. Wells." Gary grinned. "Somebody's mighty fond of you." He looked excited as if someone had given him a gift.

"So it seems." I walked over to his desk. "Another unsigned card?"

Gary didn't answer right away, he just smiled. I gave him a questioning look but he said nothing. Instead, he pushed the vase full of white calla lilies toward me with his wide smile fixed in place. I put the mail on the counter and read the card.

'Determined to get my two cents in...' signed S. Nelson.

I ran an imaginary finger through my mental rolodex. Nelson, Nelson? Where had I heard that name? Despite being a common last name, it sounded familiar to me but I drew a blank. No faces came up to match the name, nor did the first name make itself known. Samuel? Simon? Steven? Before I contemplated another batch of names, Gary broke into my thoughts.

"Turn the card over." I looked at Gary and then flipped the card to look at the back. There, on the bottom, I saw a phone number. "Are you going to call?" Gary asked, breaking into my thoughts again.

"Uh, yes. Yes, I need to. Should this be a client—which it most likely is—I need to thank them and also tell them to stop embarrassing me with these displays." I gave a short laugh.

"Between you and me, Mrs. Wells, I don't think a client is sending you flowers like these every week to say 'thank you.'"

"No?"

"Take it from a man who put much effort and thought into wooing his wife." He winked.

My thoughts raced. *Who in the world could be interested in me?* I had not even paid enough attention to notice.

Once again, I scanned my mind for faces, omitting names, trying to recapture any signs I may have missed or ignored. Norman Wright came to mind with the strange way he'd ogled me at the Mathieson shower. *Nooo!* I looked at the signature again as I walked back to my unit. S. Nelson. Would he use a false name to throw me off? I didn't see him as the cunning type, but then again he is a lawyer. I made no other connections.

Placing the flowers on the breakfast bar, I took a moment to admire how beautiful they were before reading through the mail. I wrote a check for each bill, one by one, as I opened the envelopes. The last envelope, however, I hadn't noticed until I'd sorted through the rest. It'd come from that bank again, the bank I didn't know about. However, the envelope hadn't been addressed to Skylar, or to his office, but to the Wells Family at our home address. I almost threw it away, thinking it was just another advertisement, but its stamp marked urgent in large red letters on the front stopped me.

I read the notice in disbelief. Skylar had a safe deposit box with the bank and I knew nothing about it. It said someone needed to retrieve the contents upon receipt of the notice. Why would he keep this a secret from me?

I couldn't process the information right away, but my curiosity had been piqued. I got dressed, wasting no time with hair or make-up, and dashed out the door. Once in the truck, I punched the address into the navigation system and scurried off. It took about twenty minutes to get there. Westwind Bank & Trust, a tiny local bank, had just a few locations, none of which existed outside of California. I spoke to the branch manager and showed him the notice I'd received and we took turns explaining our cases. Skylar had listed me on the safe box in addition to citing me as the beneficiary, in case of a situation such as this. I had formed a habit of carrying around Skylar's death certificate when I first lost him. Officiates wanted it for everything, it seemed. I cringed when the bank manager asked for it. He must have noticed because he apologized and carried on about procedure.

Once we'd handled all the paper work, he retrieved the secondary key—since I didn't have one, and took me to a room full of locked boxes. After locating the numbered box he'd been looking for, he put both keys into the locks. Before unlocking it, he asked if I needed a room and I'd decided I did since I had no idea about the contents of the box. He carried the large box to a tiny, nondescript room and placed it in the center of a small white table.

"Take your time," he said as he left the room, closing the door behind him.

My hands shook when I reached for the green metal box and I couldn't make them stop. The lid creaked open as I lifted it and my eyes filled with moisture before I'd seen anything inside. I wiped them away with the sleeve of my shirt.

Inside the box, sitting on top of its other contents, sat a letter with my name on it. On the front of the envelope, in Skylar's extraordinary penmanship, he'd written my name: Echo Adeline Wells. No way could I read it here, not now, so I put it to the side. Other contents of the box: a neat stack of large manila envelopes each closed with a golden metal clasp. Skylar never left anything out of place, not even in a box that no one would ever look into. At the very bottom of the box, I noticed one of his old T-shirts. I pulled it out, feeling something wrapped in its folds. I moved the fabric aside, letting it drape onto the table. My mouth fell open and I stared so long that I had forgotten to take a breath. A short cough escaped me and the noise pierced the quiet of the room, considering my breathing hadn't even lent an ambiance.

Bundles of one hundred dollar bills, piled in neat stacks, sat on the shirt. I could not even speculate how much money it amounted to. A myriad of questions swarmed my mind. I felt confused and then afraid...afraid to sit there any longer than necessary. With trembling hands I wrapped the cash back into its sheath and placed it at the bottom of a canvas tote bag I'd grabbed from the truck at the last minute. I put the money into the shopping bag as though it would break if I handled it with less than delicate fingers. Everything else I placed on top, double checking to make sure I had removed all contents from the box before closing it. I got up to leave, trailing a thank you to the manager as I hurried out the door.

I made it home without remembering the drive and all but ran to my door, rushing in to sit down so I could exhale. The air in my lungs came out in a quick rush, as if they'd been punctured, the moment my bottom hit the chair. I just sat there with the bag on my shoulder, keys dangling in my listless hand, staring at nothing. I had trouble even formulating questions. I *always* had questions but I needed to snap myself out of it. Shaking my head, I tried to rattle my brain.

As though I'd just become aware that time existed, I looked at the clock. Oh, no! It was almost eleven o'clock, and Kennedy would arrive in an hour so we could get our day started. I headed towards the baby's room to stash the entire bag. Considering, I'd always sent Kennedy in there to put things away, I hadn't opened that door in months. The sight startled me. Color samples covered the wall because Skylar and I had never made a solid decision on which color to paint the room. In the far right corner of the room, a growing mountain of sealed packages spilled out into the middle of the floor. I couldn't believe how many there were.

I remembered sending the crib back the moment I saw the picture on the box. The delivery guys tried to argue their case against my request, but between my mammoth sized tears and vehement insistence, they relented, despite protocol. My near belligerent hysterics had sent them packing. They didn't even ask me to sign anything, as I knew they should have.

I put my loaded bag on the top shelf in the farthest corner of the closet. Large boxes crowded the floor. Good grief! If I kept throwing things in there, the room wouldn't be a room anymore, but a jam-packed, half-painted, storage space. As I left the room, I looked back, promising myself

I'd sort through the mess soon. Maybe I could talk Kennedy into helping me. Her presence would make it easier to get through, for sure. Shutting the door behind me, I took off to the closet to dress. I chose a pair of relaxed gray slacks and paired it with a black top, ruffled at the hem. I pulled out a pair of flats for now and sling backs for later. While I rushed through my makeup application, I heard the door open and close.

"Kennedy, give me eight minutes! I'm just finishing my makeup—I'm already dressed," I yelled but all remained quiet. Kennedy was never quiet.

"Kennedy?"

Quiet. I stopped moving—hadn't I heard the door? I scampered to the front of the condo but saw nothing out of the ordinary. Everything looked just as it should. Could I be losing my mind? I noticed the quiet because, once again, I'd held my breath. I looked around once more before allowing myself to breathe. In the middle of my inhale or exhale—not sure which—the front door creaked open. My eyes bulged from their sockets and I froze in place. My feet felt as if they'd melted into the concrete floor. I couldn't move.

"Rise and shine, Echostien!" Kennedy shouted.

When she saw me, standing still as a stalk a few feet away, her smile went flaccid.

"Echo?" she whispered, something else she almost never did.

I could not discern if she had knocked on the door as she always did, or if I'd heard the key moving the lock aside. I clutched my stomach and folded in half, relief washing over me. It was all I could do not to crumble to the floor. *What's happening to me?* I'd started to feel a little nutty and a lot paranoid. I saw Kennedy's feet hesitate, looking as if she wanted to approach me but unable decide whether she should or not. Her movements were slight, making me feel as though I'd imagined that too.

"Breathe, honey, breathe…" I heard her say. "You look as if you've seen a ghost. What happened?"

At last, she got close enough to touch me and put her hand on my back. I stared at her black patent leather pumps and in an instant, my muscles relaxed and everything reeled in a fast motion, trying to catch up to time. I straightened up, looking into her concerned blue eyes for the first time but I couldn't speak. She slid a chair under me and I plopped down into it.

"I—I swore you were here already…I heard someone come in the door," I said, having found my voice. "I yelled for you, but you didn't answer. I stood here feeling crazy when you came through the door. I don't know what's wrong with me. I've been so jumpy—I…"

"Honey, I think you just need a vacation. We've been working nonstop for months, even on Sundays— which I haven't been happy about, by the way. You haven't been anywhere since the last time we all went to Jamaica. How about we take a girls' trip? Spend a weekend in St.

Thomas or something."

"Yeah, maybe." I glanced at the clock. Time hadn't waited for me to gather my sanity. "We've got to get going."

I sprang from the chair and ran into the bathroom to finish my hair, drawing it up off of my neck and securing it with a clip.

"Wow, another bouquet, huh? When are you going to stop holding out, Echo, and tell me who the mystery man is?"

"I'm not holding out. I don't know who it is."

"Then who is S. Nelson?" She waved the signed card in the air as I walked back into the living room. I must have looked guilty because her eyes narrowed when she looked at me.

"These came just this morning, and I haven't had a moment to figure out who that is."

"Sure." She dragged the word out. "And the phone number on the back? I suppose you haven't had time to call either?"

"No."

A devious grin spread across her face. I knew that look too well.

"No, Kennedy!" I commanded before she could say anything.

"Oh, come on!" She stomped her foot like rebellious child. "Do it for me. Even if you don't want to know, I do and if you won't call, I will!" She picked up the phone.

"Fine! Fine!" I yanked the phone from her hand but wouldn't admit to my curiosity. I rolled my eyes while she flashed a victorious smile. After punching in the numbers on the back of the card, the line rang once and someone picked up.

"Thank you for calling The Glass Oyster. Can I make a reservation for you today?" A young man's voice came on the line. I thought I'd misdialed. "Hello?" he called.

Kennedy gestured for me to say something but my confusion blocked the words that should've been coming out of my mouth. The Glass Oyster? Kennedy snatched the phone from my fingers.

"S. Nelson, please," Kennedy looked at me, widening her eyes. "Ms. Wells," she answered into the phone before jamming it back into my hand. "You're on hold...and don't you dare hang up!"

While I waited on the line, one piece of the puzzle fell into place. The Glass Oyster is the restaurant on the Santa Cruz wharf. I didn't get the chance to put anything else into perspective because someone else came on the line.

"Seth Nelson, speaking."

That's it! The restaurant owner! *He's* the one who sent flowers every week?

"What?" Kennedy mouthed, moving closer to my face.

The recognition must have registered in my expression. I plucked the card from Kennedy's slender fingers, reading the words written on the front again.

"Hello?" he said.

"Uh, yes, hi."

"Is this Mizz Wells?"

"Yes, how did you know?"

"I remember your voice," he paused. "I wasn't sure you'd call, but I must admit, I'm pleased to hear from you. How have you enjoyed your gifts?"

"Very much, thank you. You have been quite generous—"

"I hope it wasn't too forward of me or out of line," he interrupted.

I still didn't understand his motive and how had he gotten my address? He spoke again, answering my question as though he'd read my thoughts.

"I thieved your address from the comment card you filled out. There was no way I'd forget such a beautiful name or face. I hope you don't mind."

Kennedy stood close to my side, listening to every word. She'd peeled the receiver away from my ear so that we'd both be able to hear Seth. It reminded me of when we were teenagers, eavesdropping on one another's conversations.

"No, no it's fine. I actually thought you were one of my clien—" Kennedy pinched me. "Ow." She glared at me with wide eyes.

"What?" I mouthed. She made some gestures that I couldn't interpret.

"Are you okay?" Seth asked.

"Yes, I'm fine." I poked Kennedy in the shoulder.

"I must not have done a very good job if you thought one of your clients sent those gifts." He chuckled. "I figured if I remained anonymous it would better my chances of getting my two cents in...not sure if that worked in my favor."

"It seems I'm always insulting you, doesn't it?" I didn't expect him to answer, but he did.

"Well, you could make it up to me by having dinner with me on Sunday..." He paused, waiting for me to respond.

Did he just ask me out? I hadn't noticed his interest. I remained silent.

"Sure." Kennedy answered in an almost believable

imitation of my voice. I wanted to push her right over the bar.

"Great! I'll pick you up around seven, is that a good time?"

"Y—yes." I narrowed my eyes at Kennedy.

"See you then, Mizz Wells."

He disconnected the call before I could say another word. Kennedy was positively giddy. I, on the other hand, had trouble pinpointing one emotion: Confused, incredulous, shocked.

"Oh my God, you have a date! I can't believe it. I thought this day would never come. Echo, what are you going to wear? We have to find you something incredible. In the meantime, we have to get out of here. Honey, we have work to do."

She threw some last minute things into my attaché case and shoved me out the door. From then on we were in constant movement. We ran errands, picked up merchandise, and prepared the venue for our event. I couldn't believe we'd gotten everything ready on time, considering how late we'd started. Kennedy had transformed a boring ballroom into a wondrous landscape of fabric, color, and crystal. Had I not helped, I wouldn't have thought it possible to make the room so beautiful. It didn't look like the same space.

The event turned out well, and whatever hiccups

we had, the clients were oblivious to. So, in their eyes, the party had been flawless.

Our clients for the evening had conducted a successful merger and were having a lofty celebration. Rob Sellers and Darren Marik, owners of independent marketing firms, had come together to make a lucrative convergence, now called Sellers & Marik Marketing. For a bunch of office stiffs, they were a wealth of fun. We mingled with them, finding it hard not to join the festivities.

We didn't mind hanging around, even after we were done working. These guys weren't having the typical office party and it didn't look like any office party I'd ever been to. By the time these guys threw in their celebration towels, time had neared three a.m. The guests left happy, but the hosts were most happy. So much so that Sellers put us on alert for a private event and gave us a generous bonus check. Looking at the amount of his tip brought back earlier visions of the hidden stash of money in my condo. I'd almost forgotten about the morning's events concerning Skylar's box of secrets. I slipped into reverie, replaying the scene in my head, seeing the stacks of cash and the letter. I hoped to remain coherent long enough to read it when I got home. A light slap on the rump snapped me out of my thoughts, and I saw Kennedy a couple of steps ahead of me. I fell into step behind her, saying final goodbyes for the night to Sellers—Marik had made a drunken exit some time ago.

On the way home, I struggled to keep alert while Kennedy talked in a slow drawl, at least for her. She dropped me off and when I stepped foot inside I wanted to collapse right there at the door. I undressed, leaving my clothes in a heap at the foot of the bed and began dreaming before my head hit the pillow. No surprise, my dreams included Skylar. I dreamt of the time we went to Phoenix, Arizona for a basketball game. One of the players had been a patient of Skylar's when he'd started to build his reputation as a sports physical therapist. I'd been so proud of him.

I hadn't paid much attention to the game and for good reason. Skylar and I had a language all our own, filled with signs and gestures that spoke to us and confused others. We'd spent the game making googly eyes and blowing kisses at each other. A couple of times, he'd left his station, pretending he had some important, job-related task to do, when he'd actually sneaked off to steal a real kiss from me. Sometimes we'd both disappear, away from the multitude of eyes and find a semi-secluded spot to feed our carnal passions. Once, we were bold enough to christen the locker room showers of the opposing team, moments from exposure. Upon returning to our posts, we were too giddy to mask our guilt, my blushed and spotted skin, a dead giveaway.

Morning came much too soon and so did Kennedy. I'd been in such a heavy slumber that I'd neither heard Kennedy's arrival nor felt her get into bed with me.

"Wake up, Echo-cup," she whispered.

She ran a single finger down the length of my nose.

I felt one side of my mouth flash a crooked, half smile. For a brief moment, before my eyes fluttered open, I envisioned us as kids. We'd lived in the same neighborhood and had had free reign to each other's home. Kennedy had always been an early riser; therefore, she served as my alarm clock. She would bounce in, her smile in place, ponytail swinging behind her, and eyes twinkling with mischief. She often came up with some silly yet endearing nickname to wake me with, and it made me wake the same way every time. We would lie in bed together laughing and giggling at nothing, reminiscing on the previous day's mischief and all the trouble we planned to get into that day.

My eyes came open and, just for a second, I saw a twelve-year-old Kennedy, long red ponytail slicing through the soft color of the pillow, bright eyes reflecting the sky's brilliance, freckles dotting a path across both her cheekbones and over the bridge of her nose. Her rosy lips looked color stained, even then, framing a smile like sunshine.

"Mmm, morning," I said around a stretch.

Kennedy came into focus. She wore a pair of pressed, violet short shorts, a lacy, white top and a pair of four-inch heels, as if she needed help making those legs look endless. She'd slicked her hair back into a single ponytail reminding me, even more, of her as a young girl.

"How long have you been here?"

"A few minutes. Now get up! We've got things to

do."

"What are you talking about?" I ran a list of events through my head, none of which were scheduled for today nor tomorrow. "We don't have anything today."

"Oh, yes we do! Your date, hello? Get up! You have a date tonight with the hot restaurant owner. Is he hot, by the way? You never told me any details, woman!"

I couldn't believe I'd agreed to go on a date. Then I realized, I hadn't. Kennedy had. Ugh! I did not feel ready at all for a date. *I'm not going.* I thought.

Kennedy shook me.

"Wha—' I started.

"Is he hot? You never said." *That's because I hadn't noticed.* I thought. "We have to find something for you to wear. I'm thinking something relaxed, but ravishing. Maybe, a pump instead of a heel. Get up, we're going shopping."

She pushed me out of bed.

"I'm not going," I said with as much authority as I could muster.

"Yes, you are! You can't cancel. This could be a great business connection. He's got a restaurant...on the pier," she sang. "Besides, it's too last minute to cancel now."

She knew how much I hated last minute cancellations, in particular, after having made preparations.

Maybe, I could find a way to get through this, because I knew Kennedy would not relent, considering how sore a loser she could be; therefore, she ensured that she never lost. Fording my thoughts before she began her spiel, I came up with a deal. I needed to get something out of this because she'd already begun to enjoy this way too much.

"I'll go, but under condition only." She looked at me through skeptical eyes, but waited for me to finish. "Here's the deal," I paused. "You take the Tremont event on Tuesday…"

I waited. Kennedy closed her eyes as though she'd just heard a guilty verdict. The Tremonts were a frequent, but ultra-annoying client of ours. They teetered between the two of us, depending on their mood and needs. They were demanding, hard to please, worrisome, and, to be frank, a little anal. Kennedy gritted her teeth and I took that as tacit compliance.

"Thank you, Lovey!" I kissed her cheek and hopped out of bed.

Invigorated about winning her over, I skipped to the bathroom. I'd live my Tuesday as a free woman. While Kennedy, no doubt, huffed about our informal agreement, I showered and dressed, putting on one of my favorite vintage tank tops.

We made a day of shopping, browsing a few boutiques, and having lunch in Union Square. I had all but forgotten the purpose for the outing. The weather had been perfect; holding at a steady temperature of seventy-three degrees with plenty of cool breezes. I noticed that I hadn't had any reservations about driving around in Kennedy's convertible and hadn't even taken pause before getting in. Not a bad day at all, but oh, how fast the evening had descended. We pulled up to my building a little after five p.m. and made our way to my unit, leaving cheery chatter in our wake. Kennedy said she'd enjoyed my company so much that she couldn't bear to leave right away. We both knew the truth; she wanted to make sure I didn't back out, also, she wanted to lay eyes on one Mr. Nelson.

At seven p.m. on the dot, Gary buzzed me and informed me that I had a guest in the lobby, Seth Nelson.

"Thanks, Gary. Tell him I'll be right down," I said into the intercom.

Kennedy couldn't contain herself. She didn't escort me downstairs the way she'd hinted at before but, instead, went down before me, to get a good look at him. I promised to call her the moment I returned home. We— and by we, I mean she—put together an ensemble from the day's purchases, some black, slim-fit denim jeans, open-toed shoes, and a racer-back top. I wrestled my hair into a curly ponytail, each curl fighting for space, and grabbed a small clutch on my way out the door.

When the doors opened, I saw Seth's back but he turned almost the instant I stepped off the elevator. He looked more relaxed than he had at the restaurant, in a pair of jeans, yellow polo shirt, and dark blazer. His eyes widened.

"You look exquisite, Mizz Wells." He took hold of both of my hands and kissed my cheek.

"Oh, please stop calling me Ms. Wells. It's Echo, unless you want me to call you Mr. Nelson?"

"Oh God, no! Please, call me Seth. The only people who call me Mr. Nelson are bill collectors."

A giggle escaped my lips, surprising me. His smile hinted at satisfaction. Seth ushered me through the door, and I caught Gary giving me a little wink out of the corner of my eye. I did not want to think on that, just get through the night. He helped me up into his jeep and closed the door.

"I've already chosen a restaurant, but if there's anywhere you'd like to go, just say the word. Although, I think you'll like the place I've selected," he said.

"Whatever you've chosen is fine. I'd sooner trust your judgment than mine."

He chuckled. We chatted the entire way to the restaurant, making the ride feel short. He never told me where we were going, but when we got there, I couldn't wait to go in. He'd chosen a place I'd been wanting to try for some time.

Dinner went well and I couldn't believe the ease of conversation and how easy it was for *me* to talk. We didn't discuss past lives, children, or relationships, and I could not have been more grateful. We spoke about work, travel, food, and ambitions. Towards the end of dinner, I noticed how often I'd smiled. Then I realized my smiles had been the aftertaste of laughter. We had both laughed a lot. At some point, Seth had produced a single white tulip. I glanced at it gracing the dividing line on the table between us. I must have smiled again.

"What's funny?" he asked. "Share the joke, please."

"Nothing, I just looked at the tulip you gave me. As if I needed more flowers." He smiled. "Do you do this for every woman who insults you?"

"Not usually." He framed his words around a laugh. "I save the grand gestures for the really offensive."

The waiter came back to ask if we needed anything. Seth turned to me to inquire. I shook my head. I suppose the waiter had become a bit impatient, for we had long ago paid the check but were still chatting. A few minutes later, we gathered to leave. Seth took a scenic and slow route back to my house and I didn't mind since I'd been enjoying his company. We sat in front of my building for a time, continuing our conversation.

"So, would I be pushing my luck if I asked you out again?"

"Yes, you would." A smile played on my lips. "But I'll allow it this time."

"In that case, Echo, would you do me the honor of

going out with me again?"

"Yes, I've enjoyed this. Thank you."

"You're very welcome. Though I think I'm getting the better part of the deal. You are delightful company."

I thought of Kennedy and how *she'd* gotten the weaker part of deal and laughed to myself. Seth and I didn't decide on anything right away, but agreed to speak the next day, after we'd both had a chance to check our schedules. A true gentleman, Seth walked me to the door.

"Truly a pleasure," he said, kissing my hand.

He handed me the tulip and takeout box of my leftovers and didn't pull away from the curb until the door had closed behind me. Gary sat at the security station, grinning like a Cheshire cat. I didn't want to speak to him for fear that he'd ask a barrage of questions. Kennedy would, for sure, fulfill that destiny later.

"Goodnight, Mrs. Wells," Gary said. Thank goodness he didn't say anything else.

"Goodnight, Gary." I kept moving towards the elevators.

Hearing Gary call me Mrs. Wells made me think of Skylar for some reason, not that he'd ever called me anything else. I toyed with the ring roped around my neck and smiled at a thought of him. Then I remembered the letter I had not yet read. As soon as I got inside, I pulled down the bag from the closet, my hands shaking again. I pulled the letter out first and unfolded the paper as if the words would fall off the page if I weren't careful.

Echo, my love. I fear that the reading of these words means I have suffered a fate that has left you to live a life without me. I'm sorry, love, to have left you so soon. Know that I never took you or your love for granted. You have my heart, even in my absence. I didn't think it were possible to love as fervently as I love you and that I would receive that same love in return. It's quite befitting that your name is Echo. You are my Echo. You are more than I'd ever dreamed. I feel as though I'm the one who has been blessed beyond measure to have lived and loved in a life that includes you.

The contents of this box are a compilation of surprises that I'd planned. Don't be angry that I kept this from you. I know how much you hate secrets, but you love surprises. Of course, I never intended for you to find out this way.

First surpise: I bought a loft for you. It's so you'll have a place to paint, to create. Your own space, your own art gallery. It's in Soma. It's being renovated and remodeled by a man named Santiago Ruiz. I've paid him in advance to get the work done. I want you to have everything you've ever dreamed; it's only fair since you've given me the same. Inside is all the paperwork and documents you'll need.

The other surprise is a savings bond for the baby. I want to make sure he has everything we had and everything we didn't. You are going to make a phenomenal mother. The final surprise is some money I'd put away for you to use however you see fit. Launch your gallery, spoil the baby rotten...live! I just wanted to take care of my two greatest loves. I know you're wondering where it all came from. Bryant gave me some stock and investment leads, some of which paid off.

I love you, Echo Wells, and you too, Little Wells. You'll forever be my Love's Echo. Find happiness...for you have plenty of it to give and you've filled me to overflowing.

Always and Forever

Your Beautiful Morning,

Sky

Teardrops splashed onto my arm. Skylar still had the power to amaze and awe me. I refolded the letter, placed it back inside the envelope and pulled out one of the large manila envelopes, marked "Surprise!"

Sure enough, I found a deed and documents for an address in Soma, accompanied by pictures and keys. Skylar had paid for the space in full as well as the taxes for five years. That's why I had not known. He'd thought of everything. From the looks of the pictures, the place had been in shams. The loft looked as though it needed lots of work; bringing to light another reason I had not yet been contacted by the contractor. He had more than enough work to keep him busy for well over a year. The permits and reconstruction alone would amount to months of waiting, not to include the months of construction to follow. I couldn't believe he'd done such a thing for me, although it felt bittersweet without him to share it with.

Smiling at the thought of him, I sifted through the bag some more. I imagined the expression he'd wear while delivering such an enormous surprise. I found more sealed envelopes, each marked on the front in Skylar's handwriting as a clue to its contents. One said: "Savings Bonds," another read: *"Finge Inc."* and another had been marked: "Bryant."

Bryant? Why would there be an envelope with Bryant's name on it? What could be so special, so sacred that he'd kept it the locked box? What needed protection as much as the things he'd given and written to me, his wife?

My movements had become sluggish. I seemed to move slower with each passing minute. Even my thoughts had slowed down. As much as I wanted to know the details of every folder, I couldn't continue. Replacing each item back into the bag, I once again, placed it into the far corner of the closet and shut the door. I put my single tulip in the vase with my lilies and my leftovers into the refrigerator. Then, retrieving my phone from the tiny purse I'd been carrying, I checked it for missed calls and messages. Kennedy had called twice already. I bet she thought I was still out with Seth. Stretching across the bed, I called her. The phone didn't sound a full ring before she picked up. I pictured her sitting there with her thumb on the answer button.

"So, how'd it go? Tell me everything, spare no details. Where did he take you? It must've been a good time because it is late. He is hot stuff! Tell me, tell me!" she carried on.

Late, it couldn't be more than 10:30. I looked at the clock to find that midnight had come and gone. It felt as if I had just gotten home.

"Hellooo? Details, woman!" she demanded.

"Alright already! Do you remember that place I've been dying to try, on Folsom Street?"

"Yes, the one you won't shut up about?"

"Azie. Well, that's where we went. He was a complete gentleman. I have to admit, I enjoyed myself. At first, I just tried to get through it, but he seems like a nice guy."

"So are you two going out again?" I heard the smile in her voice.

"Yes, but we haven't picked a day yet. He's going to call me tomorrow."

I heard Bryant's voice in the background, but couldn't make out what he'd said. I assumed he wondered what had Kennedy fired up at such an hour. I thought back to the folder with his name on it. Tomorrow, tomorrow I'll open it.

"Kennedy, I'm turning in. I had no idea it was so late."

"Ok, hun. Bryant's complaining anyway. Night."

"Night."

We hung up. I kicked off my shoes and lay there staring at the ceiling. After a while, I stripped down to my underwear and shoved myself under the tucked covers.

*F*our

*S*leep came without hesitation and brought with it a new dream. My belly protruded with new life, taut and round. Skylar stood behind me whispering something unintelligible. A smile spread across my face and felt his wide hands on either side of my belly. He'd covered my eyes with a cloth and with one arm wrapped around my waist, he came to my side. I heard his smile, felt his excitement as he guided me inside, feeling the change in temperature. He unlocked a door.

"Are you ready?" he asked, taunting me.

"Yes, yes, yes!" I all but jumped up and down. He fiddled at the back of my head, releasing the blindfold.

"Surprise!"

My eyes widened and shimmered with tears. I stared at a large room with aged brick walls on every side, thick wooden beams and columns holding the structure steady, weathered floors that had stood the test of time and taken a beating. Tools had been strewn all over the place as and dust and years of airborne debris clouded windows.

"Well, what do you think? Of course, it's not done yet, but I couldn't wait any longer. Besides, I want you to have a say in how it turns out." I didn't answer. "Baby, say something."

Too choked up to say anything at all, I remained quiet. He hugged me from behind and I could feel his triumphant smile on the side of my face.

"Your very own art studio," he whispered, kissing my collarbone.

He rested his chin on my shoulder. After a few seconds, I turned into him to kiss his lips, taking a moment to stare into his eyes. I leaned into him and just before our lips met, my eyes opened and a tear escaped. That dream would never make its way to reality.

In the shower, I tried to wash away the maelstrom the dream had left behind, hoping it would swirl down the drain with the sudsy water. I wasn't very successful. I dried off and dressed and headed into the kitchen. Starved, I ate my leftovers from last night for breakfast. While I sat at the bar, shoveling the food into my mouth, a white envelope slid across the polished floor from under the other side of the front door. I jumped up as fast as I could and yanked the door open but didn't see anyone, nor did I hear any sounds of footsteps. Nothing. I peered down the hallway and into the stairwell but saw nothing. I went back inside, picking up the blank envelope and reseated myself in front of my plate. Unfolding the single typed page inside and putting a forkful of food in my mouth at the same time, I read the words.

The food caught in my throat midway down. My fork fell to the plate and then clamored to the floor. I let the paper drop to the counter as though it had been coated with disease. I coughed…hard. The half-masticated food had blocked my airway. I ran around to the sink and guzzled water straight from the tap. I couldn't recall if the food had come up or gone down. I rushed out the door as I tried to catch my breath.

I hurried to my SUV, looking around in every direction. I threw my briefcase and the letter onto the passenger seat and locked the doors upon closing them. I felt safer in the cabin of the Volvo, but I had to get out of the parking lot, away from my house. I drove out of the lot and into morning traffic casting suspicious eyes on cars driving by and then eyeing the people inside. At a red light I glanced over at the letter again. The page contained one question: WHAT 'S IN THE BOX?

I arrived at my office in record time, all the while trying not to think about the question. It didn't work. I didn't know which frightened me more: the fact that someone knew about the box or that they were hand delivering inquiries asking about it. At first I wondered, "what box?" as I thought of the many crowding the spare room but that couldn't be of much significance. As far as I knew, it was just a bunch of baby items and care packages for a grieving widow. Dismissing that thought, I figured it had to have something to do with the safe deposit box. Considering the amount of cash inside, that made more sense. I hadn't even known about it, so who the hell else could have known enough to ask? My best friend didn't have any knowledge of the box, let alone anyone else.

"Kennedy," I said aloud, picking up the phone and punching in her office number.

"K. Keigle Designs," a pleasant and cheery voice said into the phone.

"Kennedy, please," I barked.

"May I say who's calling?"

"Echo."

"Oh, hello, Ms. Wells. It's Sherri, how are you?"

"Hi, Sherri, is Kennedy around?" I ignored her question. I hadn't meant to be rude but I didn't have time for small talk.

"Sure thing, hold on."

Sherri had been Kennedy's assistant for years and still I'd never picked up on her voice. To me she sounded like every other receptionist at every other office.

"Kennedy Keigle here." She came on after a short hold.

"Kennedy, it's me, Echo."

"Hey, sweetie, what's up?"

"Are you free for lunch today? I need to talk to you."

"Anything for you. I'll shuffle some things around. Meet me at that café you like on Sanchez & Duboce, 12:30."

"Ok, see you then." We hung up.

Calling Kennedy at her office guaranteed a short and normal paced conversation. While I waited for lunchtime to roll around, I busied myself with details of the Tremont event. I had to smooth out every detail so Kennedy would have the least amount of trouble with them. I'd been poring over each detail for the third time when my line buzzed.

"Ms. Wells, you have a call on line two, a Mr. Nelson," the receptionist said.

"Thanks." I pressed the blinking button on the phone. "Well, hello."

"Good morning, Echo. How goes it?" Seth greeted. Muted clatter filled the background, cluing me in to his whereabouts.

"I've had an eventful morning and yourself?"

"Not too bad. I hope eventful means good," he prodded.

"I wish it did."

"Well, you can talk to me if you need to get some things off your chest. I promise not to tell. Scouts' honor." In my mind, I saw him hand gesturing the boy scouts honor pledge.

"You're very sweet. I'll keep that in mind."

"Echo Wells?" I looked up to see a delivery guy standing at my office door with a vase full of yellow tulips.

"Yes," I answered.

"Sign here, please."

The man approached my desk and set the vase down on an empty corner. Once I'd signed, he gave a simple nod and disappeared without another word. Seth had been so quiet on the line, I thought he'd hung up.

"Hello?" I called.

"I'm still here."

"You have got to stop!" I smiled. "I have another embarrassing display here...embarrassing, but beautiful."

I had enjoyed the attention and looked forward to seeing the splash of color in my otherwise drab office space.

"Are you telling me you don't like the flowers? I could send chocolates, oversized teddy bears, or singing and dancing telegrams," he teased.

"No! Please don't! I do like them," I admitted. "By all means, send these if the alternative is grown men in costumes singing juvenile poetry."

We laughed. A minute later, we were discussing our upcoming date. The word "date" sounded strange to me. I wasn't sure I wanted to call it that. We compared schedules, and I mentioned that I had the next day free, leaving out the part about it being a bribe. He told me he had some tasks for the early part of the morning, but that his afternoon was also clear and we agreed to get together around noon. Realizing that I'd never given him my phone number, I offered him my cell number and thanked him for the tulips. In turn, he thanked me for agreeing to see him again and we hung up.

After going over the Tremont file for the fourth time, I put it all together and placed it inside my attaché case to give to Kennedy at lunch. Time flew by as I managed other details for a few of the other events cramming my schedule. I'd been so absorbed in my tasks that lunch time crept up on me. It felt as if it'd just been thirty minutes that had gone by. Time had been whizzing by a lot.

Kennedy had already grabbed an outside table by the time I'd arrived. Two steaming mugs sat on the table, an indication that she'd ordered something for both of us. She hadn't ordered food which I appreciated since I still felt stuffed from my near gluttonous morning meal.

"You sounded tense on the phone. Is everything okay? Did the hot blond guy mess up already? What did he do? Do you know where he lives, because I'll kick his ass?" she reeled, wasting no time at all.

I kissed her cheek and sat down across from her, taking a slow, timid sip of my cappuccino before speaking.

"No, I wish it were that simple. Seth is doing just fine, but it's nice to know you'll go around beating up grown men for me." We giggled. "There is something much more important I need to discuss with you." Before she could interrupt, I kept talking. "I found out that Skylar had a safe deposit box," I held up a hand to keep her from running off at the mouth, which fell open. "In it, he'd written a letter to me with some other documents, but I haven't gone through all of them yet. Kennedy, he bought a loft...for me. He said it's so I can have my own gallery."

Kennedy's eyebrows sprang up. She sat quiet for a moment but I knew it wouldn't last long.

"Echo, oh my God, that's great! I just wish he were here. You've dreamt of this for so long." I wish he were here too. "Well, where is it? When are we going to see it? How big is it?"

"There's more," I stated, before she interjected another stream of questions. Her face incredulous, she scrunched her brows together. "A while back, I got an unmarked letter in the mail. Inside, on a single sheet of paper, someone had typed a question: 'How much do you know?' This morning another note slid under my door."

I pulled out the note and handed it to her. Kennedy's eyes went wide as she read the words.

"What...? I don't understand. Who else knows about this?" she asked.

"No one. I hadn't even told you."

I hadn't decided how much to tell her. In most cases, good or bad, we'd lay out all details for one another, but this felt different. Although Kennedy had proven herself trustworthy over the years, I couldn't bring myself to let her in on all the details and telling her about the "Bryant" file, considering I didn't know what it contained, was out of the question. It could be nothing but it could also spell trouble.

She looked at the note again and shook her head. I guessed that she'd struggled to make sense of it all, as I had been.

"Have you gone to the police?" She looked up from the paper.

"And tell them what?" My voice went up a few octaves. "An imaginary friend is sending me questioning letters? It's not like they've threatened me. What would be my claim? I don't even know where the notes are coming from."

She shrugged her shoulders as she shook her head.

"Well, was there anything else in the box?"

My stomach churned with emotion. I took another long sip of my drink, feeling the heat as it splashed into the pit of my belly.

"Money," I whispered.

"Ok, how much?" Her tone rang with indifference.

"A lot."

Kennedy shrugged her shoulders while a look of impatience crept onto her face.

"What's a lot? A few grand, ten, twenty, what?"

"I haven't counted, maybe a couple hundred."

"Thousand?" Disbelief flashed in her eyes.

"Mmm-hmm." I took another sip.

"Where did Skylar get that kind of money?"

"In the letter, he mentioned that he'd made some investments that paid out. He wanted to surprise me. He also bought savings bonds for the baby and paid a contractor to renovate the loft."

"Wow, Skylar, I'm impressed. Well, you need to count the money and put it somewhere safe. Bryant has a bill counter at home—"

"No!" I cut her off. "I don't want him, er, anyone to know about this. I'm freaked out enough." She looked astonished by my outburst.

"Okay, okay, no Bryant. I'll just sneak it out of the house and we can count it at your place."

"I'm sorry. This whole thing has me edgy. Can we change the subject now, please?"

"That's easy, tell me about Chef Hottie." Her eyes twinkled with anticipation.

I told her more about the night before, about the additional bouquet of flowers he'd sent, then I handed her the file I'd put together for Tremonts.

"It's a good thing you're handling this event..." Her face went flat. "Because Seth and I are getting together tomorrow afternoon."

I felt an impish grin form on my face and she stifled a scream even though I'd given no other details. It didn't matter, however, she'd been excited enough.

We both went our separate ways after lunch. My day and night flitted away with busy tasks, and before I realized it, Tuesday morning had arrived. Knowing Seth would be on time, and eleven o'clock had already come and gone, I showered and dressed without lingering too long on one or the other. Just as before, Seth hadn't revealed our plans for the day so, I donned a pair of jeans, an off-the-shoulder top and a pair of sandals. It felt like a pretty safe bet. As expected, my intercom buzzed at twelve on the nose.

"Ms. Wells, a Mr. Nelson is in the lobby for you."

Trevor's voice came over the speaker.

Trevor, a much younger guard, wasn't as personable as Gary.

"Thanks, Trevor. Tell him I'll be right there."

"No prob, Ms. Wells."

After locking the door behind me, I stuffed the keys in my pocket. Seth stood waiting at the elevator doors when I stepped out and held his elbow out to me.

"Shall we?" He bowed. I smiled at his chivalrous display and hooked my arm through his as we walked outside. "You look beautiful, as always."

"Thank you."

"I thought we'd take the trolley down to the pier... is that okay?"

"Yes. It's been a while since I've taken the trolley."

"Great."

Thank goodness I'd worn comfortable shoes. We walked for a while before hopping on the trolley, still hooked at the elbows. Taking my time, for a change, felt nice. Once we boarded the trolley, we sat close together and continued to converse. The ride seemed longer than I remembered, but Seth had been such good company, I didn't mind. During the ebb and flow of passengers, Seth had given his seat to a woman with the prettiest little girl. He stood in front of me while I made funny faces at the chubby, rosy cheeked little girl with fatted arms and legs. The sight of her made me want to take a bite of her chunky limbs. She wore a tiny pink bow which secured the wisps of hair atop her head. Her deep set dimples and smile melted my heart without remorse. I played with her, delighting in her uncontrollable laughter until she and her mom got off.

My tangled emotions couldn't decide whether to laugh or cry. My heart broke into fragmented pieces on the inside, but I didn't want to freak Seth out so I contained my tears. Except, not all of them stayed put. One rogue drop escaped the corner of my eye. I swiped it away before Seth could see; though, he didn't often take his eyes from me. I tried to concentrate on the joy this precious little girl had shared with me. Her contagious giggles didn't just make me smile, she'd made others smile as well. I'd felt a little sad when they exited.

By the time Seth and I got to the pier, we were both hungry. We dined at the Rainforest Café but our conversation wasn't as light and careless as before.

"Why were you crying earlier?" he asked. "I saw you wiping away tears. The baby wasn't that cute." He chuckled.

I wasn't as stealthy as I thought I'd been. I foraged through my mind, trying to create a crafty way to answer his question without lying or telling my entire, tragic story. However, I couldn't determine how much would be too much...not for him, but for me. I had no desire to talk about the accident. That wound still had not scabbed over yet, although I could feel some healing taking place. Stymied, I gave the simplest response I could come up with, hoping it wouldn't prompt him to ask even more questions.

"I lost my baby about a year and a half ago." I looked down at my plate.

"Oh, I'm sorry. I didn't mean to pry or bring up bad memories." He stammered around his next few words, seeming unsure of how to proceed. "Let's—let's talk about something else."

Whew! Relief washed over me and my muscles relaxed, appreciative of the subject change. After dinner, we walked off our meal on the pier and had ice cream as we sat watching the waves roll. I learned a lot about Seth throughout our long afternoon together. However, he couldn't say the same about me. I let him talk and though I listened, I didn't interject many additives from my personal life, he didn't appear to notice. We popped into a few art galleries, and I found myself plucking ideas from each about how I'd like my gallery to be.

By the time we headed back, the sun had begun to set. The trip back to my place went a lot faster. He walked me to the door and kissed my cheek. Inside, Gary had replaced Trevor for the evening shift and got a bird's eye view of the innocent kiss.

Over the next several weeks, Seth and I had gone out often, and he'd still send me flowers, but never a singing telegram, thank goodness. Once I'd gotten comfortable with him, I'd revealed that I'd been widowed, sparing the details of how it had happened. He seemed satisfied with the little information I'd given him. I appreciated that he'd let me move at my own pace.

Whatever had grown between Seth and me had become comfortable. Whether to label it a friendship or a relationship, I couldn't figure. We spoke as friends, but dated enough to consider what we had a relationship.

Few other things had changed. I hadn't received any more letters or inquiries from the invisible writer but Kennedy and I had, however, counted the money. She gasped when I unwrapped the cash. Though we weren't strangers to large sums of money, having cash in such a quantity, close enough to smell it was different. It felt a lot different from seeing the zeros in your bank account or on a check and touching the money with your bare hands.

The sum came up to almost half a million dollars. We both almost fell out of our chairs, $472,208 to be exact. We hadn't figured out what to do with it yet. We assumed the money hadn't been taxed, touched or, as far as we knew, traced. Too much to put anywhere at once without raising suspicion, we decided against putting in my bank account. Even if Skylar had legally attained the money, it would look fishy. Also, whoever knew about the box, had some knowledge about the money as well.

Counting the money had renewed my curiosity in the files I had yet to open. One evening, since I'd gotten home at a decent hour, I decided to go through at least one of them. I began with Bryant's, opening the envelope and sliding the contents onto the table. Skylar had kept a handwritten log of meetings he'd had with Bryant. Also, he'd kept record of meetings between Bryant and a company called *Finge Inc.*, each catalogued with date, place, and time. After skimming the pages, I moved on, reading just enough to get an idea of what he'd included. One page contained figures, numbers, and dollar amounts. Other pages were full of stock language and terminology. It may as well have been hieroglyphics for all I understood.

Skipping to the last of the contents, I found pictures, a number of which included Bryant at various locations, with different people. One man in the photo had been present in almost every picture. I couldn't understand what it all meant. As I flipped through the papers, a few colorful post-its flittered to the floor. I picked them up and thought of how many more pieces there could be to this evolving puzzle.

Most of the notes were questions regarding the people in the pictures. One in particular questioned the figure most constant with Bryant's image. In one of them, Bryant and another man made an exchange; what's in the case? I read some other notes he'd written, raising more questions that didn't have any answers I could see. *Great,* I thought, *as if I needed more mystery to my life.* The more I read, the less I understood. I became confused and confusion begot frustration and frustration, annoyance. I slammed the papers down and huffed, pouting like a spoiled child. Determined to figure out at least one iota of the jigsaw, I opened the *Finge* file.

For the sake of my intelligence, I needed to put one piece in its proper place. The *Finge* information proved more of the same, pages of it. Scribbled on multiple notes were questions and indefinites: 'Where are they?' 'No address found.' 'No return on investment.' 'Company not found.' Some pictures corresponded with one another while others were different, but often contained the same people. Just as before, a note slipped from between the pages. I stared at it on the floor for a moment before picking it up. It looked a lot like the notes I'd received which had no distinguishing properties. That, however, was just it, having nothing to trace or compare it to, except for its lack. Inside, I saw a single typed demand: STOP DIGGING.

As if the instructions had been the exact opposite, I turned on the computer. I felt defiant, like someone who's told what to do but does the opposite instead. Also, my husband had found suspicion among all this, and I wanted to answer all the questions he hadn't had the chance to.

While the computer booted, I made some tea. I had forgotten about the kettle until it began its whistling siren. Back at the computer, I typed in the company name in the Internet search bar. Compared to what a mainstream company's results would be, the results for *Finge Inc* were few. I clicked on the links, but they were all dead-ends. Some websites were under construction, others unfound and more still redirected to irrelevant pages. *What the hell?* I thought. Irritation fired my determination. I clicked on every result, switching midway from tea to coffee. What seemed like a thousand clicks later, my eyelids grew heavy and I rested them, laying my head on the desk.

The sun shone, tangerine beams into my windows. I lifted my head in response to the light, looking around the room and realizing that I'd fallen asleep in front of my computer. With a key stroke, I brought it back to life, scanning the page I'd last read. My eyes burned with deprivation of sleep as well as deprivation of answers. Before logging off, I sent the receptionist at my office an email informing her that I wouldn't be in until late afternoon and to hold all my messages.

I fell onto my bed atop the covers, leaving all my clothes on except for my shoes. The stretch of muscles felt good and I'd fallen into a deep sleep within minutes. My dreams led me to a night a few months before the accident.

Kennedy, Bryant, Skylar, and I had spent the evening together. Bryant had been designated as our driver for the night. We piled into his Mercedes Benz, Skylar and I in back, and drove farther into town. That night, we went to a modern adaptation of Shakespeare's *Othello*. The guys had not been excited about it, but the same couldn't be said for Kennedy and me. At least we hadn't made them suffer through the ballet; we'd spared them from that and went together instead.

We all had talked over each other in the car. I don't know how we'd ever started, finished, or deciphered a conversation between us, but somehow no point ever got lost in the fog of verbiage. For any onlooker it appeared as mild chaos. Then, as if on cue, we would all erupt into laughter or state a joke's punch line in unison. We carried on until the lights in the theater dimmed. Sometimes a whispered joke would make its way from one end of our group to the other, like a stadium wave, contagious in its flight. Hushed snickers hovered between us and the irritated glares of other patrons added to the mirth. We'd all been familiar with the story of *Othello*; otherwise we would have missed plenty of pivotal moments considering our behavior.

Afterwards, we'd gone for a late dinner. Having had such a formal evening, we'd opted for the most informal eatery. We went to a tavern called Jack's Juke. The place wasn't pretty, but they had astounding food. The long wooden bar had a butt on every stool, every time we went. The wall behind the bar had been crowded with liquor bottles, inches from the ceiling, in various stages of empty. An antique jukebox sat off to the side, boasting rainbow lit colors that danced with the music. Each song played from the surface of vinyl 45s. Hoping for the most current music would be a waste of energy.

The atmosphere had always been so dark, it made me wonder if the lights worked at all. Tiny, red, beaded dresses covered bulb-shaped candles centered on each table. We'd found a rounded booth as far left as we could go and seated ourselves. Sliding into the booth, the darkness provided some relief from seeing the stains on the seat. All the tables and chairs were dark brown, except the booths, which were a deep shade of red. The floor had been a mystery to us all, having never seen it. We'd kept a running bet of what we thought the floors may have been made of, each choosing a different material.

Squinting at the menus, printed on food stained paper, we had placed our orders with Lynn, a young waitress who didn't look old enough to serve or drink alcohol. She looked pretty ticked off, either because we had been there or she had to be. Each of us had ordered a drink, except Bryant, keeping the good times going.

Our food had come sooner than it seemed it should have. Skylar had ordered a gargantuan burger with more dressings than I'd known existed. I wouldn't have been able to get my mouth around it for a bite, but he just about inhaled it. The rest of us had a medley of deep fried dishes.

Stuffed to the hilt and just an ounce shy of tipsy, we headed back to my and Skylar's place for a nightcap, as if we'd needed more to drink. I, for sure, didn't. I seldom drank alcohol, so the effects had felt extreme. The three of us had strutted around the condo with glasses of wine in hand, giggling at things that had seemed funny and some things that didn't. It hadn't been clear who talked to whom and even less of whom had been listening.

Skylar had disappeared into the bathroom for the fourth time during the course of an hour. Kennedy and I rummaged through my closet, for what, I had no clue. When Skylar had emerged, his shirt stuck to him in various places, he couldn't tell us how he'd gotten wet. I threw him a clean, dry t-shirt to put on and for some reason, we'd found this funny because we laughed much harder than necessary. We'd gone from almost tipsy to almost drunk. We returned to the living room, stumbling over our jovial howling, back to where Bryant had been left alone and sober. Kennedy and Skylar had been too busy falling over each other to notice Bryant's wary expression. I saw him through the open door of the office and walked over.

"What are you doing?" I asked, around a chuckle, pushing the door open.

He stood there looking like a home invader whose owner had just turned on the lights. The desk drawer in front of him had been opened and sifted through, disrupting Skylar's orderliness.

"Uh, looking for a pen. This would be a logical place to look, don't you think?"

His dark eyes shifted back and forth to points beyond me. Given my altered state of awareness, I hadn't thought much of it then and ignored the fact that he'd been holding our checkbook in his hands.

"There's a container full of pens right there." I pointed to the cylinder next to the computer monitor, brimming with a multitude of writing utensils.

He looked at them with a sheepish expression and made a scoffing sound. Replacing the checks, he retrieved a pen and bumped the drawer closed with his hip. I don't remember ever seeing him use the pen. Little time passed before Bryant rushed his drunken wife out the door, leaving Skylar and me to our own devices.

The liquor had not only infused us with laughter but lust and we gave in to it the moment Bryant shut the door behind himself. I can say with near certainty that had been the night we'd conceived Baby Wells. We'd awakened in a tangled heap of limbs, sheets, and pillows on the floor next to the bed. The morning sun hadn't stirred us, but our rumbling, noonday bellies roused us from an intoxicated doze.

I awoke with a slight headache, just as we had then. On the way to the office, I stopped and picked up a cappuccino and a scone. As soon as I sat down, I popped two aspirin in my mouth and swallowed them back with a scalding sip of the sweet drink. When I got to my office, a new bunch of flowers sat on my desk and a stack of messages. Kennedy had left three all her own. *Why hadn't she called me on my cell? Where is that thing anyway?* I had no idea. I searched through my case and purse but came up empty.

"Humph." I scanned my office, searching with my eyes, as if it would materialize before me.

I'd have to look for it later, I told myself as I picked up the receiver and dialed Kennedy's office. Her assistant answered, informing me that Kennedy had stepped out. I called her cell.

"Where the hell have you been! Does your cell

phone not work? Did you lose it again? Were you held off somewhere with Seth? Is that why you're so late? You know I started to come over, but that would've been mighty unfortunate for me to walk in on your morning activities," Kennedy spouted, chuckling around her last sentence.

I could just see her air quotes around the word *activities*. When the questions began to roll, I wished I'd waited until she had gotten back to the office. I would have been able to avoid this stream of questions.

"Hi, Kennedy. No, I wasn't with Seth—"

"Damn! I hoped you had been. So what else could've kept you out until mid-afternoon, if it wasn't Chef Hottie? He would be much more worth it than whatever you were doing."

"I wasn't feeling so well this morning. In fact, I still have a headache." I'd hoped that would be enough justification to pacify her.

"Ugh! That's it?" she scoffed, her disappointment apparent. "A girl can dream...moving on. Don't forget we've got a meeting with Mr. Ruiz in a couple of days to see the loft. Oh, and we're having drinks with a pair of business partners from Amber's shower at nine tonight at the Ritz."

The Mathieson's shower seemed like ages ago, although it had just been a couple of months. Hearing her name again reminded me of the birth announcement they'd sent me. They'd had a baby boy named Dean Andrew. He had diminutive features, like his mother and dark hair. For such a tiny woman, she'd delivered a pretty big baby. He'd been eight pounds, two ounces and, of course, she was already back to her petite self.

"Do you want me to pick you up?" I heard Kennedy ask.

"Sure."

The drink meeting went well and we were able to put yet another team event on the books. If we kept it up, I'd be spending my nine to fives at her office or she at mine. Our team dynamics kept roping everybody in. As long as they kept loving us, business kept flowing, a winning situation.

Friday came fast. I had double timed to get paperwork filled out and vendor incidentals set so that I could take as much time as I could to view the loft and, maybe, run some ideas by the contractor. I had no idea what Skylar had drafted nor did I have much of an idea of what I wanted. By late afternoon, Kennedy and I had pulled into the gated lot. I felt a trifecta of emotions: joy, sorrow, disbelief. The building looked beautiful; that is, if you liked centuries-old brick and old world craftsmanship.

The structure wore its age with pride like a teenager, earmarking ever year closer to legal, boasting to the younger generation. Ivy grew out of nothing to climb the east outside wall, painting over the tan colored brick with its lush green. The front door, made of heavy, dark wood, had been carved with an intricate, undecipherable pattern. We entered through the garage, an open space, much larger than average, interspersed with supporting metal poles. Heavy footsteps trotted down the stairs and a moment later a man, whom I presumed to be Mr. Ruiz, rounded the corner.

Five

"Ms. Wells?" he called.

"Yes, Mr. Ruiz, I assume."

"You are correct."

By now his long strides had brought us face to face. He held out his hand and I shook it, all but forgetting about Kennedy, who'd been so quiet.

"And you are?" He offered his extended hand to her.

"Kennedy Keigle." She shook his hand and I noticed her doe-eyed expression.

What's wrong with her? I thought.

"Nice to finally meet you, Ms. Wells." He turned to me. "So sorry about Skylar, he was such a genuine guy."

The mention of Skylar's name and the fact that he'd known about his death caught me off guard. I didn't know what to say.

"Thank you," I managed. Kennedy still hadn't said a word. I stole a glance at her when he'd turned his back to us.

"What's your problem?" I mouthed.

"He's beautiful!" she mouthed back, doing sign language for the word at the same time.

I rolled my eyes, shrugged my shoulders, and shook my head all at once. Unable to pinpoint the reason, but something about her annoyed me just then.

"Mr. Ruiz?" I called.

"Please, Mr. Ruiz is my father. I'm Santiago. We have no need to be so formal. Besides, I've heard so much about you, Ms. Wells, I feel like we're friends."

"Okay, Santiago. Well, feel free to call me Echo then."

I'd expected Kennedy to interject her own informality but she never did. Santiago gave us a brief tour of the basement and garage, showing us hidden storage areas and closet spaces. Then we continued upstairs. I took a deep breath as I looked around. It looked similar to the one I'd dreamt but I loved the tangible version much more.

"Excuse the mess." He stepped over a tool. "Watch your step. There's always work to do; therefore, there's always a mess." He paused. "Echo, are you alright?"

I wasn't sure what he'd meant.

"Huh?" A heavy release of air whooshed out of my mouth as I spoke. "Uh, yeah. Sorry. It's spectacular!"

"Do you need some water or something?" He looked unsure of me, as though he didn't believe I was okay.

"No, I'm fine. Really." I turned to Kennedy but she wasn't next to me where I thought she'd be.

"Well, here she is. Annabel, the project from hell." He chuckled as his admiring eyes darted around the huge space. "She's a beauty."

"I agree." He turned to me, disbelief written on his face. "What?" I asked, feeling self-conscious under his gaze.

"Few people see the beauty and character of a space like this until all the handy-work is done and the fancy bells and whistles are in place."

"Not me."

"That's a first, but Skylar knew you'd like it."

I thought of him then, trying to find the perfect

place for me to create. I could see his face smiling, his eyes sparkling when he happened upon this place. The space felt open and airy, despite the mounds of sawdust. A sawhorse sat in the middle of the room and the gutted kitchen exposed the plumbing behind the walls.

"Take a look around," Santiago urged. "It's yours."

As if I'd needed the command to move, I walked forward exploring the sectioned rooms. Most of the materials that separated the two bedrooms were all new. The common areas were divided by a staircase, separate from the one that led to the basement and garage. I walked up the stairs to the loft area where a balcony stood out from the rear, showcasing an amazing view.

"So?" Santiago's voice came from behind me. He dragged out the single syllable to make an entire sentence out of the word. The sudden sound gave me a start. "Sorry, I didn't mean to startle you."

"I think I'm in love," I said, more to myself than to him.

"Yeah, Annabel made me fall hard too."

I hadn't needed to turn around to recognize that he'd smiled. His smile sounded as audible as his actual voice.

I liked the way the loft felt, the way I felt in the loft. It felt as if happiness could be born here. After I had taken the tour and imbibed the space and its details, I talked to

Santiago about what I wanted. He showed me prints and design ideas that he and Skylar had come up with. Some I loved and others I'd pushed aside for my own personal touches.

He had kept the original flooring, which I loved, maintaining the integrity of the structure. He had made numerous repairs and modernizations, which, he'd informed me, weren't complete yet. We agreed to meet again the next day to pick out toilets. *That should be fun*, I thought. Except not. He walked me down to the parking lot and shook my hand again.

"Nice to finally meet you, Echo. See you tomorrow."

"See you."

Kennedy—already seated behind the wheel of the car—started the engine before I had even closed the door. Her behavior struck me as odd. At some point, she opened her mouth to talk, but I wasn't listening. I think I heard every seventh word. I daydreamed about the loft. What I would put where, fixtures, and faucets. We'd arrived at my place in no time, but Kennedy didn't bother to come up, for which I was grateful.

The next morning, I awoke with some extra pep. I couldn't believe my excitement about looking at toilets. I walked through the parking deck to my truck, but pulled up short a few feet away. Graffiti stained my front windshield. Someone had written a message in white paint:

WE KNOW ABOUT THE MONEY.

I gasped and looked around at the lot full of cars. Scared, I ran back upstairs, not knowing what I would do, but something came to me the moment I stepped inside. I grabbed the bag of money, leaving the documents in the closet for closer inspection later. Then I found my old passport and jammed it into my shorts pocket. Last, I took some things from the kitchen: a knife, a scouring pad, and a bottled water. I headed back to my truck and took out my phone—which I'd found crammed in a fold of the couch—to call Santiago to tell him I'd be late, when I thought of something else. Standing in front of the truck, I snapped a picture of the message with my phone. Tossing my things onto the seat, I then scrubbed the glass, getting it as clean as I could, crying while I scrubbed.

On my way to the loft, I stopped at the last bank I saw before getting there. Using my old passport, I got myself a safe deposit box. Instead of putting it under my married name, I thought I'd put in under my maiden name: Echo Green. After pining over that for a minute, I thought better of it. Using Green might still make it a bit too easy to find me, if someone wanted to. My mother had been gracious enough to bless me with four names. I had added to the pot when I'd gotten married. Not many people knew my middle names, apart from Kennedy and Skylar. With that in mind, I'd decided it best to use both my middle names, one of which is my mother's maiden name: Adeline Eberhardt. She had wanted me to remain tied to her Germanic roots, and I could not have been happier for that more than at this moment. Satisfied that I'd outwitted my stalkers,—at least for now—I headed to the loft.

I hopped out of my car, spewing apologies to Santiago, who'd, though accepting, told me to shut up in a roundabout way. He had started working on the wall with the exposed pipes while waiting for me to arrive and asked if I'd mind waiting while he finished. I agreed.

"How are you?" he asked. "Are you okay?"

"Yeah, why?"

"When you first got here you looked flustered and upset. I know you couldn't have been that jarred about being a little late."

His observation took me aback. I hadn't thought it obvious, and I, for certain, hadn't expected him to call me out on it. Without thinking about it, I started talking, finding him easy to talk to. Too easy. I began blabbing about what had happened on my way over and even told him about the strange letters. I'd left out the parts about what the letters had said or that they'd been hand delivered. It wasn't until I'd closed my mouth that I realized I'd said too much.

I'd just blurted it out this privileged information to a stranger. Even though I'd left out most of the details, telling him about someone leaving a message on my window had been more than enough. Considering that I had not told anyone about the situation and even Kennedy only knew scrambled pieces, I understood why my mouth had run away with me. I needed the release. He listened while he worked, asking a question every now and then. I sat on the floor with one leg folded underneath me, talking in a very matter-of-fact way. It wasn't long before he'd finished sealing the wall and we headed to the home improvement store.

While he locked up, I made a beeline to my SUV. As I pulled on the handle I heard Santiago clear his throat. I looked over and he stood holding the door open for me. The door to his old, dirty, beat-up work truck. I figured it used to be white; though, it boasted a shade of dingy. It had a rusty frame and dents seemed to be a part of its façade. A discolored towel covered the single, long, front seat and a rosary hung from the rearview mirror. Tools littered the seats, front and back and if the inside was that unkempt, I'd hate to see the monstrosity that lay in the truck's bed. I gave a mirthless laugh.

"You don't expect me to ride in that?" I pointed a condescending finger at his disintegrating pick-up.

"I sure do!" He looked at me with hard eyes. "There's no way we're going to fit three toilets in that thing." He mocked me by pointing at my SUV.

As much as I'd hated to agree with his logic, I had to. I huffed over to his truck, where he still held the door open, as if he knew he'd win the argument all along. I tried to lift myself into the truck, but slipped. He caught me under my armpit and lifted me into the cab.

"Thanks," I mumbled.

He didn't respond but walked around to the other side, got in, and slammed the door shut. He scowled as he mumbled under his breath and I watched as his face turned red and I swore I heard him call me pretentious. Since I couldn't be certain of what I'd heard, I decided against a response to keep from putting my sneakered foot in my mouth. He kept his eyes on the road and said nothing to me which I found annoying though I couldn't figure out why. To distract myself, I played with a stray thread at the hem of my shorts and pulled non-existent lint from my shirt.

When we arrived at the store, he all but jumped out of the vehicle, barely slamming it into park first. His strides took him halfway across the lot before I'd even gotten out. I pulled on the handle and the door fell open with a loud creak. I swung my legs around and felt for something solid with my foot. Even though I didn't have firm footing, I hopped down anyway. Bad idea! It was a longer way down than I'd anticipated. Trusting my own calculations had turned out to be disastrous. When I slid off the seat, a sharp piece of the truck's frame caught me on the way down, cutting into my flesh. I felt the metal as it dug into my thigh and yelped at the pain as I came down hard on my feet, causing my knees to buckle.

I saw Santiago's feet in the distance come to a halt mid step. Blood seeped down my leg and onto my hands. I had not even noticed he'd turned around until I felt his arm behind me supporting my weight. I drew my arm around him to sustain myself. He kicked the door shut without even looking at me while rambling audible but indistinct foreign expletives. He helped me hobble into the store and demanded someone get a first-aid kit. An employee brought one out along with paper towels and plastic gloves. I watched the scene as though I wasn't a part of it.

"Oh!" I gasped. Santiago had hoisted me onto the counter, taking me by surprise.

"Do you need some help, sir?" One of the managers asked.

"No!" he growled. "This is my project; I'll handle it."

Project? I was his "project" now? Offended into silence, I just sat there as he cleaned the blood off of my thigh and bandaged my cuts. He about snatched me off the counter afterwards.

"Are you okay?" He still wouldn't look at me but busied himself cleaning up the wipes, wrappers and paper towels he'd used and the one I'd used to wipe my hands.

"Fine," I said, my tone terse. I didn't bother to thank him.

We made our way through the store, but now Santiago hovered closer, perhaps from fear that I'd lose a limb by tripping over a saw or something. He should've just wheeled me on the giant metal pushcart with the merchandise. That would have made it easier to keep an eye on me. I scoffed at the thought aloud, even though I didn't mean to. His head snapped towards me, but he didn't say anything.

Once we got down to business, his mood seemed to lighten. I figured that had nothing to do with me and much more to do with all the tools surrounding us. He looked as though he belonged in the store with his tattered shirt and paint-stained jeans. *Why in the hell did he have on a tool belt?* What was he going to do, build a tree house in the middle of the store? My internal comments came out as a snicker prompting Santiago to turn towards me but he turned his head a fraction of the way in my direction and then forward again. I looked down at his boots, spattered with various substances and concluded that yes, he definitely belonged here.

His mood turned apathetic as I mulled over what type of toilet I wanted to sit my bum on. After choosing three, one for each of the bathrooms in the loft, we moved on to handles. We spent hours in the store, picking, choosing, and debating over one thing after another. I could not comprehend why we were debating over something that wasn't his choice. The loft belonged to me but oh, that's right, it was his project and apparently, so was I.

I hadn't planned to spend my entire day picking out toilet seats, especially not with such a temperamental sourpuss. We'd filled the pushcart from end to end by the time we were done shopping. Though I wouldn't admit it out loud, Santiago had been right. No way would we have gotten half that stuff into my Volvo. However, that didn't mean I'd been any happier about riding in his dingy deathtrap. I probably had rust poisoning from the gash his jalopy had given me. To prevent further injury, he'd made certain I was inside with seat belt fastened before loading up all the goods. He did the same when we returned to the loft. I didn't need to go inside, so I got into my truck and left.

When I got home, I once again pored over the words and numbers of the mystery files, trying to piece things together. I looked at the log and compared them with the notes. Between the two references, things began to make more sense. The first entry had been noted as Bryant and Skylar at the gym. It hadn't struck me as important enough to document since they'd always worked out together but Skylar's notes told a different story. The day he'd logged had been the day Bryant had talked him into investing in *Finge Inc.* Bryant had never tried to convince Skylar of any such thing before, as far as I knew. Considering that Bryant worked in that market, I'm sure Skylar figured he wouldn't steer him wrong, at least that was my logic. So, from the looks of it, Skylar had taken his advice.

Another entry stated a meeting Skylar had with a lender. *That's what that was about!* I remembered him mentioning something of that nature to me. Skylar had known that number talk pretty much went over my head, something, I guess, he'd counted on. He'd borrowed fifty-thousand dollars and invested it instead of delving into our savings. From what I understood, according to the log he kept, he'd doubled the money the first time, repaid the loan, and reinvested a few times more. Each time yielded a more lucrative sum than the last. For a while, all the investments paid out, but then the log changed formats. He'd stated investments, but no returns and then nothing at all. Skylar logged neither investment nor return.

From there, all meetings were between Bryant and others. Skylar had opened an account at the bank where the safe deposit box had been, and his notes read that someone had emptied it by using an untraceable wire transfer. I'd always marveled at his foresight and it had not failed him this time. He'd thought enough to put some of the money he'd made into the box, making it untouchable, even to the bank. That would be the money he'd left for me.

Clipped to an invoice. I found the business card of a private investigator, Mark Shuler. He must have been the person who'd taken all the pictures. I made a mental note to contact him on Monday. The sheets of numbers were still a mystery to me, but I'd begun to understand the other pages.

I wondered what Bryant had been up to. For sure, Skylar had the same suspicions. I couldn't see Bryant being money hungry; he and Kennedy did well for themselves. Then again, so did Skylar and I, but that had not stopped him from making secret investments. Besides, we were all friends, right? My head had started to throb at all the new information. Information, I had no clue what to do with. I couldn't say anything to Kennedy because I wasn't sure how it would affect her, or guarantee that she wouldn't blab to Bryant. I wondered if she'd told him about the box or the money, I hoped not. I didn't know how deep or how shallow this murky pond was. I'd better hope it was shallow or learn to swim in the infested waters. Something's wrong here. Skylar knew it and, now, so did I.

After a while, I put the files away and took a shower, changed the dressing on my thigh and crawled into bed, mentally exhausted. My wound blazed red, surrounded by bruised skin...how attractive. Still quite tender, I rolled over to my other side and fell into a restless asleep.

Back in the car with Skylar again, he talked to the unborn child in my womb. We progressed through the green traffic light, laughing together. Neither of us noticed until it was too late. A large white van had sped through the intersection, plowing into us. The impact smashed the door in with incredible force where Skylar sat, his hand still on my belly. The airbags deployed and shattered glass dispersed in every possible direction. The van had been moving so fast that it pushed our car sideways, causing it to slam into another moving vehicle, crushing my door in as well. Something pierced into my right thigh and an instant later, another jolt dislodged my seat. The object that had pierced my thigh sliced through me as the seat slid back on its rails. All the noise—yelling, horns, sirens, and frantic conversations—made it almost impossible to hear my own screams. I grabbed my thigh and looked left for Skylar.

"Sky," I cried out but he didn't answer me.

My vision had gone blurry. I could see shapes and

fuzzy looking objects, but couldn't make anything out. I reached for him and felt his arm, but he wasn't moving.

"Sky?" *Why wouldn't he answer me?* "Sky!"

I heard him groan and my heart sank with relief. I had a hard time breathing. Why couldn't I breathe? The blurriness intensified and the noise quieted a little and then a lot. I became less conscious of my surroundings, but still felt Skylar's arm, warm under my hand. I heard someone calling my name, but it wasn't Skylar's voice as I had hoped. I opened my eyes for a moment but couldn't quite make out the figure, the face in front of me. My vision sharpened for a split second and I thought I recognized the face but just as fast as my eyes opened, they closed again and all the noise, even the familiar voice vanished.

The next time I opened my eyes everything had changed. Flowers and balloons were everywhere and I heard a chirping sound, an incessant beeping. My leg hurt, seared with pain, but so did everything else. I felt weighted down. Trying to focus, I looked down. Large leather straps kept my wrists and ankles fastened to the rail of a hospital bed. Why in the hell had I been tied up like some mental patient? I strained against the cuffs to no avail. *Could somebody untie me and get this damned tube out of my nose!* The words never came out of my mouth. Had someone tied that too? I lay still for a minute, using all my mental power to concentrate. What had happened?

My stomach threw a violent cramp around my insides. I groaned, the sound painful to my ears. I heard movement and when I looked over near the window, I saw my mother. She rushed over to me but I couldn't understand why she'd come and even less why I'd been tied to a hospital bed.

"Hi, sweetie," Her German accent saturated each word. I tried to speak. "Shh, shh, shh, don't talk. I'll get you some ice."

She ran a cube of ice along my parched lips first, which gave them permission to open. Then she fed me one ice chip at a time. I felt confusion clouding my eyes. After a while, I tried to speak, each word coming out in a croak. I didn't recognize my own voice.

"Mum..." Her eyes were so sad. "Mum," I chocked out again.

Just then Kennedy walked in carrying an armload of fast food bags. She wasn't her usual overload of good tidings. I'd been hospitalized before and she'd always cheered me up but it didn't look like that would be the case. Her eyes looked strange to me, they weren't their usual striking ice, instead, they were a dull cloud of blue. *What in the hell had happened? Was I dying? Who*—I couldn't complete another thought.

"Where's Sky?" I asked.

My mom looked away so I looked to Kennedy and noticed her wet eyes. I cleared my throat, ignoring the pain. Maybe she hadn't hear me.

"Where's Skylar?" I croaked louder.

Moisture fell from her eyes and my mom still hadn't turned back to me. Kennedy shook her head. *What the hell did that mean?*

"Where is Skylar?" The beeping of the machines had increased, agitating me more.

"He didn't make it," Kennedy whispered, her voice fading.

I strained to hear her. Didn't make it where? Where did he go without me? I didn't understand. I looked from Kennedy to my mother, but neither said anything more.

"What do you mean? Where did he go?"

I felt frustrated, my words garbled, but I knew she understood me.

"Echo..." Kennedy sat opposite my mother who cried too. She touched my restrained arm. "Skylar..." she paused, attempting to clear her throat. "Skylar didn't make it out of the accident alive."

"Wh—what?" I huffed. My eyes burned and bile rose in my throat. But—I, we—"

I couldn't form a sentence and, all of a sudden, I understood why I'd been bound. I wanted to buck like a wild bull. I felt every muscle in my body tense and strain to the point of pain. My back arched as far up as my spine would allow and a howl came out of my mouth that didn't sound human, let alone mine. Heat flushed my face, making my tears burn. Then it felt as if I'd wet myself, liquid streaming between my thighs. I let out a piercing scream.

"Shh, honey, or they'll medicate you again," someone said.

I threw my head from side to side and tears seemed to flow from places other than my eyes. Nurses rushed in. I heard their clamor and Kennedy and my mother arguing with them. I screamed Skylar's name, but he did not answer. My hysterics broke into uncontrollable, violent sobs. I wanted to cover my face with my hands, hide my eyes from all this, but I could not. While they cleaned up all the blood, I cried still.

Sometime later, for which I had no reference, someone untied me. I lay there stoic but then I remembered we had a baby. I clutched at my belly and opened my mouth to speak. Before the words had even formed in my mind, I saw my mom shaking her head. I didn't scream. Instead, I curled into a ball and cried until it hurt. Then I cried some more and more still after that. *How had I lost everything? Why hadn't I gone too?* I wanted to be with them.

———————

My face still felt hot when I came into consciousness. My wet pillow cooled one side of my face from the tears I'd shed during the night. It had been a long time since my dreams caused me to cry that way. Revisiting the past via what Skylar had left behind had forced me backwards, but also fueled a determination to figure out what had driven him to such high suspicions and out-of-character behavior. I felt the tears at my lashes and on my cheeks making me wonder how long I'd cried. I got up and went to the bathroom, catching a glimpse of myself in the mirror. The appearance of the person looking back at me was startling. It looked as though I'd been sunbathing, laying out in the sun a little too long. I splashed water on my face to relieve the internal fire but it made little difference, so I went to the kitchen to get an icy drink of water. Then I heard urgent knocking at my door.

"Just a minute," I called, while running to grab my robe. Looking through the peephole, I saw Trevor on the other side of the door. He looked worried when I opened the door. "Trevor—"

"Ms. Wells, are you okay?" He interrupted, peeking around me. He hadn't given me a chance to answer. "Some of the other tenants said they heard a woman's screams coming from your unit."

As he awaited for my answer, I flushed with embarrassment.

"Oh. Um. I'm sorry, I had a nightmare." Trevor looked me in the eyes, making me feel even more uncomfortable.

"Are you sure everything is okay, Ms. Wells? You were just dreaming?" He looked behind me again and then back to my eyes.

"Yes, Trevor. I'm fine, embarrassment aside, of course." He seemed to relax a little. "Just," I paused. "Just don't tell anyone, okay?"

"You have my word, Ms. Wells." He walked away, but not without a final glance around.

I closed the door behind him and picked up my water glass, drinking it down at once. I glanced at the clock. Shoot! Seth would arrive in ten minutes! I decided to wear jeans instead of, well, anything else, considering I had a fresh gash the size of Tennessee on one thigh and a matching scar the size of Texas on the other. I didn't want Seth to see them, even more, I did not want to have to explain them either. As I pulled on my jeans, I ran my finger along my healed scar, feeling where the tissues had regenerated, making the scar raise up a bit from the flesh.

The door buzzer pulled me out of my trance. Seth, of course, had arrived at the exact hour he'd said he would. Damn him for being so punctual! Couldn't he be late for once, like a normal person? I pulled a t-shirt over my head, yanked on some socks, and hopped on one foot to the buzzer trying to put on my boots.

"Two minutes!" I yelled into the speaker.

"You got it." Trevor sounded much calmer.

Seth and I were going to drive to Mountain View to go hiking. I'd never been hiking before, so the closest thing I had to hiking boots were a pair of work boots that Skylar had bought while we were renovating our condo and he'd insisted I wear them. I threw my hair up into a sloppy ponytail and dashed out the door, keys and phone in hand. *Did I brush my teeth?* I cupped my hands over my mouth to smell my breath. Nope. I ran back inside, did a quick brush, grabbed a stick of gum for added defense, and ran out the door again.

"Hi." I gave Seth a quick peck on the lips when I'd stepped off the elevator. "So sorry to keep you waiting."

"Don't worry about it. It was worth it, you look great."

"Thanks."

"Are you ready for this?" he asked.

"Not really, but let's go before I come to my senses." We laughed.

Seth had promised to take it easy on me, so he'd picked an easy trail for us to hike. That hadn't eased my worry, because his brand of easy and mine could be quite different. He'd told me the name of the trail, but I'd had trouble pronouncing it. Every time he'd said it, I heard: Eric Estrada. So I'd dubbed it the Estrada Trail. Seth found it hilarious and laughed, hard. He was like the awkwardly amused friend. Like the one person who finds a joke hilarious and goes to bits laughing, while everyone else gives a short chuckle and moves on. He's that guy.

By the time we got to the trail, I couldn't hide my nervousness. Clumsy by nature, Seth had taken me somewhere that would, no doubt, exhibit that particular trait of mine. I had to admit, the hike had been easy...for Seth. He glided along the path as if we were on an escalator, while I fumbled alongside him. It wasn't all bad. We had moments of enjoyment. He'd even filled a backpack full of snacks and considering my love for sweets, he'd packed chocolate covered energy bars. His pride showed and while I'd appreciated his consideration, the thoughtful little bars tasted like chocolate-covered dirt. I suffered through it in an effort not to discredit his efforts. A few hours later, tired and sweaty, the hike ended. Seth looked as though he'd taken a walk to the mailbox while I looked as though I'd climbed a mountain in summer.

He took me to a tiny restaurant nearby for a late lunch or perhaps an early dinner. I couldn't believe my appetite. Seth watched in awe as I ravenously devoured my food. He stared at me with a slight grin. Although we'd been out to eat many times, I'd never been so hungry or careless with my manners.

"What?" I stopped chewing. *Had he even eaten or had he just been creepily watching me?*

"Nothing." He smiled. "I've never seen you eat so much. That hike must have really taken a lot out of you."

No kidding. I swallowed and took a sip of water.

"It did take a lot out of me and I forgot to eat

breakfast this morning."

"Well, that explains it."

I smiled, noticing that he had not eaten very much at all.

"You're not hungry?" I asked.

I doubted he'd even broken a light sweat under his shirt, whereas I felt certain he could smell me from across the table.

"Not really, but please don't let that deter you." He gestured to my plate.

In other words, go on, eat like a pig, while I watch in feigned appreciation. I became self-conscious after that, so I pretended to be full. In truth, I would have been happy to put away a few more bites. He tried to encourage me to continue, but I felt a little embarrassed, I wasn't sure why. It could've been the way he stared that made me uneasy. The waiter boxed the remainder of my meal, and we left not long after. By the time Seth got me home, I felt the pain from the hike begin to settle into my muscles.

"We should do this again soon. There's this other great trail that I think you'll like."

I hoped my face did not reflect my thoughts. Despite the time we had been spending together, Seth had not learned much about me. Not that it had been his fault. My comfort with him had increased, but the window into who I was had not opened much. I couldn't blame the guy.

"Sure," I managed to say.

Heaven knows I did not want to do that trail or any other ever again, much less soon. It almost felt as though we hadn't been on the same hike together. Had he seen the stumbles and discomfort beaded on my face along with the sweat? Had he paid any attention at all to my body language? The answer was simple: No.

He kissed my lips, the single place on my body that wouldn't be or wasn't already sore. He had taken my hand in his as I turned to walk away, stretching our arms out between us as he let go. I smiled, looking behind me and waving with my free hand.

Once inside, I ran a bath as hot as I could stand and soaked for an hour. Despite the waterproof bandage I'd put over the gash on my thigh, the heat still seared it but I endured the pain. Exhausted, I went to bed at eight p.m., waking around three in the morning with a start. I'd dreamed of the accident again. I didn't think I'd screamed in my sleep, but then again, I hadn't known that I'd screamed the night before either. I supposed I would hear of it in the morning if I had. My body nor mind would allow me to stay awake, pulling me back into a heavy slumber.

The next morning brought with it more to do concerning Skylar's files. The first thing on my list had been to check with the Office of Corporations to see what or if I could find anything on the mysterious company I'd been trying to obtain information about. Searching the Internet had been a dead end, and phone calls didn't prove to be much more efficient.

Finding a local address for an office in town, I'd decided to make my inquiry in person. The woman operating the front desk did not look happy. She looked at me when I'd walked in, but said nothing. She wore a headset connected to a phone on her desk with several blinking red lights. Her tone sounded terse as she spoke into the microphone at her lips. At the same time, she fumbled and shuffled through paper, pens, folders, and computer data. She looked at me again and, without a word, shoved a clipboard at me to sign in. I did so and returned it to her. She took it and went back to her excessive multitasking. Taking my cue from her, I found a seat and flipped through a dated magazine. After a few minutes, she called my name. Even though no one else sat in the waiting area with me, she phrased my name as a question.

"Do you have an appointment?" she asked.

"No, I don't."

"Who would you like to see then?"

"I'm not sure. I am trying to find some information on a particular company."

"Okay, let me see who's free. Just a moment." She clicked a button or two on her elaborate phone system.

"Braum, do you have time for an inquiry right now?" She paused. "Yes, she's here in the lobby." She answered another question I couldn't hear and then spoke again to me. "Braum will be out in a moment."

I couldn't decide if Braum was a first or last name. Once inside his office, the distinction did not become any clearer. His nameplate had been printed with one name and nothing else. Braum, a short, dumpy man with receding white hair, absent in regions on his head, sat behind his wide desk. The years had not been kind to him and age spots freckled his face and hands. I sat opposite him in the windowless office.

"How can I help you?" he asked.

I explained what I needed as he punched the keys on his keyboard. Through the reflection in a pair of glasses that rested on the bridge of his nose, I saw that he'd searched one screen after another. Several times he'd asked me to spell the company name. His search came up empty and my hope had started to deflate. I knew I'd been headed for a brick wall.

"I'm sorry. I can't find anything on that. Are you certain you have the proper spelling?"

"Yes." I sighed. It's five letters, how wrong could I get it?

"Let me look in one more place."

It always sounded funny to me when someone said, "look" referring to a search engine on the Internet. As though they were physically getting up and searching for something.

"Hmm?" he paused. "I found something here with that name, but there aren't any specifics. No address, personnel, phone number, not even the type of company. These don't often make it into the system. Why is it in..." he trailed off.

By the time he finished looking, he'd found two listings for *Finge*, both very vague, so he suspected they were one and the same. One of them he'd found in archives, but he hadn't specified where he'd found the other. The one in archives had a date from four years ago and had been active for less than a year before its removal. The only name affiliated with the company had been Jahi Ali, but Braum hadn't found his position nor anything else. He'd told me how rare an occurrence it was for such scarce information regarding a company to make it into their database. He couldn't comprehend the lack of details considering the measures and provisions they'd put in place in order to maintain the integrity their system.

His minimal finds, again, left me with more questions than answers. I thanked him and left, wondering how much red tape a company had to cut through to register at the Office of Corporations or how much one could slither through. My mind ran through the list as my phone rang. I rifled through my purse and pressed the talk button before thinking to check the caller ID.

"Hello?"

"Good morning, Echo. It's Santiago." I closed my eyes, almost bumping into one of the concrete columns in the parking garage.

"Echo?" he called. I blinked, slow and long. "Are you there? Echo, can you hear me?"

"Yes, yes, I'm here. Sorry. I'm in a parking garage, the signal must be faulty," I lied.

"Oh, I could call you back."

"No!"

My answer came out fast, too fast, and too anxious. The line went quiet. I opened my mouth to say hello, but he spoke first. I closed my eyes again.

"Well, I won't keep you. I'm calling because we never set up another date for you to come up and look at the installed toilets. You also need to pick out the other faucets and sinks..."

"Wow, you're done with those already? That was fast."

"Yes, well, I put two of the three in right away. There's not much to it. Will you have any time this week to swing by?"

"How's tomorrow?" I suggested without giving any thought to what may already be on my schedule.

"Tomorrow's great. Does one o'clock work for you?" I swore I heard his voice change.

"That's fine." Ugh! I did it again! I gave no thought

to my answer.

"Okay then. See you tomorrow. I told you I wouldn't keep you."

He smiled again. *How did I know that? Is everyone's smile as audible as his?* I couldn't recall ever being so aware until now.

"Okay, see you tomorrow."

We said goodbye and hung up. I went to take a step forward, but the painted, yellow column and I were at a standoff. I had not moved an inch while talking to Santiago. At last, sidestepping the pole, I made it to my SUV and headed to the private investigator's office, hoping I'd have better luck getting solid answers from Mark Shuler than I had gotten from Braum.

Six

Shuler's office sat tucked inside a residential area. The Victorian style home had been divided into four business spaces. In addition to Shuler's office, it held a photography studio, a tiny law firm, and one unclaimed space. I took the stairs to the upper level, following the sign to his office and found his door padlocked with a litter of colored notices covering the door like paint.

Some words jumped out from the papers like, hazard; do not enter; but one phrase rose from the page as though it were in 3-D: Crime Scene. *Crime Scene?* Of course, I knew what the term meant, but asked myself the definition anyway. I began to peel back one corner after another among the many sheets. The dates on them rocked me back on my heels. Whatever had happened had taken place just days after *our* accident. Could this be related to

Skylar? I dismissed the thought. It seemed preposterous, but there had to be a way for it to all add up.

Behind me, a door opened and a teenaged boy walked out into the hallway. He had a thin physique, a low, tapered haircut and creamy brown skin. He looked at me for a brief moment before speaking.

"Hi," he said.

"Hi," I responded, unsure of what else to say.

"You don't know what happened there, do you?"

"No, I don't. I suppose you do."

"Oh, yeah." He brightened.

"Can you tell me?"

"You're not a reporter, are you?"

"No, I'm not."

He seemed to size me up one last time before deciding it'd be okay to talk to me. He leaned against the door frame as he began relaying what he knew.

"A guy was killed in there in the middle of the day! Took them three days to find his body...stunk like hell. They say he was stabbed a bunch of times." He'd been so casual, so matter-of-fact while he spoke, but my heart pounded in my chest. I hoped he couldn't hear it. "He was a detective or something. They're still looking for the person who did it, that's why all those notices are up there and nobody's rented the place."

I turned to look at the door again, the notices having new meaning, new voices.

"My mom's a photographer here." He jabbed a thumb at the door behind him. "We were gonna move, but the landlord convinced us to stay and even put in extra locks and an alarm system."

"Wow," I said. "You're not scared?"

It was a dumb question for me to ask a teenage boy, as if he'd ever admit to being afraid, to a woman, no less.

"Nah, I grew up in worse places than this."

He may not have been scared, but I couldn't say the same.

"Did they run this story in the paper?"

"Yeah, for a while. They interviewed all of us, but the other people downstairs moved, an older lady and her daughter; they sewed or made clothes. Something like that. The word is that it's some big conspiracy, kinda like in the movies." He smiled.

If only he knew how much this wasn't a movie, at least not for me. This had become more real than I'd ever thought it would be again.

"Well, thanks for talking with me." I turned to leave.

"Yeah, sure." He stayed in place, watching me down the stairs.

I hadn't noticed my hands were shaking until I went to put the keys in the ignition. I don't know what Skylar had gotten himself into. Even more, why I'd picked up where he'd left off. The kid had been half right about one thing: this was playing out a bit like a movie, because I'd never thought of this type of thing happening in real life, and I would've never thought it would happen in mine.

I drove on auto-pilot to the library as my thoughts ran one into the other. A loud shrill pierced my ears and snatched me away from my colliding thoughts. The sudden interruption caused me to swerve. I retrieved my phone and looked at the caller ID: Kennedy. She'd have an earful for me. I could not even remember the last time we'd spoken. I silenced the phone's scream and made a mental note to call her as soon as I arrived at the library. I pulled up a few minutes later, and before I'd put the truck in park, my phone rang again.

"What in the world is going on? I haven't heard from you in a week and why haven't you been to the office? Do you know how much work we have to get done? We have three events next week! Besides that, why is my best friend and my husband behaving so peculiarly? I don't understand and nobody's talking to me. What's happening? Echo! Echo?" she rambled until she'd gotten breathless.

"Kennedy, calm down, honey," I soothed, hearing the pain in her voice.

She sniffled and it broke my heart. I hated to hear Kennedy so upset. The woman didn't cry unless it'd been court ordered.

"I'm sorry I've been so distant. Where are you?"

I still didn't want to involve her any more than necessary, but I saw how the secrets were hurting us both.

"Sitting in the car a few blocks from your office. I went looking for you, but they said you hadn't come in this morning. Can you please tell me what I've done that you won't even talk to me?"

"Nothing, sweetie. This thing that Skylar left behind is...I'm just trying to make sense of it and I've gotten a little consumed." Her comment made me curious about Bryant's behavior. "You said Bryant is acting strange? What's he doing?"

"It's not what he's doing. It's what he isn't. He's coming home late, he's not cooking dinner anymore, and he won't even look me in the eye. Our conversations are strained, and he's always a little testy. He also has this growing fascination with your life..." she trailed off. I took a breath to speak, but she continued. "It's like he's...I don't know...like he's not himself...or..."

She didn't finish her sentence. Kennedy had become accustomed to getting what she wanted and needed, but right now that wasn't happening.

Kennedy, the youngest of four children, had always

been distinct even with two older brothers and a sister. All her siblings had shaded blond hair but she had a fiery red mane. Their eyes were similar in color, but hers beckoned attention with their unusual brightness and while her siblings were often compliant, Kennedy loved a challenge.

Kennedy's family spoiled her as a child, not so much because she'd been the baby of the family, but because she'd demanded it. Even I tended to spoil her. I didn't know how she did it, but she made everyone feel good about it. She'd somehow make it worth your while to give her what she wanted. Bryant had always catered to her, from the moment they met.

———————

At 7:30 a.m. at the Coffee Bean in Santa Barbara, Kennedy stood in line, tall and radiant. She wore a short black dress, belted at the waist. Her hair—shorter then—in a bob which hung just below her ears had been pressed straight, which, of course, looked stunning. Hooked on the crook of her elbow she'd had a large fuchsia-colored tote to match her fuchsia and black Jimmy Choo's. Two people were ahead of her, and one of them happened to be Bryant Ascot.

I'd sat at a table near the window, reviewing the logistics for a casting party we'd been planning for one of our college mates. We had taken the drive to Santa Barbara the day before and had been so excited we couldn't sleep. So we'd gotten a jump-start on the day, beginning with coffee. We would order the same thing every time, so Kennedy hadn't needed to mull over the menu. Bryant, however, had required extra time. He stared at the menu for an interminable amount of time, according to Kennedy. Impatient, Kennedy placed her order ahead of his, making no apologies. Bryant gave her an annoyed look, but it hadn't lasted more than a second. His glare transformed into awe. I saw a smile come out of hiding, lighting his eyes before reaching his lips.

Bryant hadn't been anywhere near Kennedy's type, upon first glance. His youth showed on his face and his head of dark hair, and his average build were both shorter than I'd known her to be attracted to. He had dark eyes and had been "cubicle ready" dressed in dark slacks, white shirt, and colorful tie. All of which seemed like strikes against him. Kennedy often went for the taller guys with a lesser sense of style, ever determined to be the pretty one. Her gravitational pull led her to surfer guys who dressed in tattered shorts, tank tops, and sandals.

Kennedy threw a raised eyebrow in Bryant's direction, daring him to object. As suspected, he did not, but placed his order with the barista as if he'd just had an epiphany. He pulled out his wallet and paid for both his and Kennedy's drinks. She gave him an informal thank you with the wink of an eye. Bryant's smile widened. Once the drinks were ready, Bryant stepped in front of her, grabbed the cups, and carried them to our table. I saw the intrigue on Kennedy's face as she led the way.

He placed the items on the table, introduced himself, and took a seat. *Bold move.* Kennedy gave me a hint of a smile. Bryant turned out to be charming, holding a quiet confidence evident in his speech. His outward appearance had suggested timidity, but he'd proved otherwise. Kennedy, surprised, became curious about him. He hadn't overstayed his welcome, but sat with us just long enough to pique Kennedy's interest. He'd left his card among our scattered papers and departed with a cheerful goodbye. Mission accomplished. I knew he'd made a lasting impression on Kennedy when she'd mentioned him several times during the day; she'd even remembered his name— first and last.

The two had begun dating almost right away. We'd double-dated some of the time, setting the precedent for upcoming years. Kennedy became schoolgirl giddy. It'd been weird to see her behave that way. She'd never been *that* girl in school. Boys would fall at her feet, and she'd step over them, taking their offered gifts without a backward glance. She'd been so different with Bryant. I could never decide who'd enjoyed the pampering most, but I suppose it hadn't mattered.

Their courtship had been shorter than their wedding planning. I still can't figure out know how Bryant had pulled it off, but he'd spared nothing for his bride who'd spent not a cent of her own money. Their relationship had remained almost unchanged throughout the years—that is until now.

"Echo, I don't know what to do, or what to think."

I heard her say, pulling me back to the present.

"Look, I'll meet you for lunch at *Ozumo* around two o'clock. We'll have sushi and talk, okay?" I suggested, thinking that would give me a couple more hours to browse the newspaper archives before lunch.

"Okay." A note of cheerfulness lit her voice.

At the library, I'd found the article on Shuler's death. It said that someone had stabbed him seven times, in his office, on a Tuesday afternoon in October. It had occurred just two days after my and Skylar's car accident. Shuler's office had been ransacked and files had been stolen and his computer destroyed. The more I read, the more it scared me. Whoever had done these things were determined to get what they wanted and silence anyone who knew anything. The article also mentioned that the intruders had left behind some evidence, but didn't disclose any further details about that. Sifting further, I found a tiny article by a freelance writer who claimed Shuler had kept a storage room, as a backup of all his clients' information. Any or all of which could had been connected to his demise.

As I read on, a name about jumped off the page, making me lose my breath the moment I saw it. Jahi Ali, his name kept popping up. In another article, the reporter referenced Raggiro, a ghost company suspected of swindling money from its investors. Ali, at one time, had been jailed for money laundering and had been a key player in the fraudulent dealings. The piece had been written more than ten years ago by a Robert Cane in one of the local neighborhood news journals. Those papers were, for the most part, printed and delivered inside one subdivision. Those were the newspapers no one paid for nor wanted. Instead, the printed pages lined pet cages or littered driveways, often left wet and soggy to be tossed in the trash bin unread. I wondered how this issue had ended up here. I wondered if it had been catalogued because it were related to a bigger story in the mainstream newspaper. I scanned the article again, plucking out relative facts. Raggiro, Raggiro, why did that ring a bell? I'd never heard of the company, but the name sounded familiar.

Scrolling down to the end, I saw a picture in the side bar. At first, I assumed it to be a picture of the writer until I read the fine print underneath. "Pictured here: Jahi Ali", the caption read. The black and white picture looked grainy and what should have been distinguishing features melded one into the other. His face appeared as more of a blur than identifiable; another nagging familiarity. Even amid undecipherable characters, he seemed a familiar face to me. The more I discovered, the less the pieces fit into the grooves of where I'd thought they belonged.

One o'clock had crept up fast, so before heading out, I did a quick search for stories related to *Finge Inc.*, but turned up very little. I learned that the company had been short-lived, having gone belly-up in August about two years ago. All the dates I'd discovered were so close to when I'd lost Skylar. It couldn't be coincidence. I tried not to let my imagination run away with me, but it was hard not to, considering the tangled web weaving itself right in front of me. I checked the time and scurried to leave, something I should have done ten minutes ago.

I breezed into *Ozumo*, spotting Kennedy at a corner table. She smiled in obvious relief. Maybe she'd thought I'd stand her up. I saw the sake on the table and wondered how much of it she'd already drank.

"Hi, cupquake," I said.

I had my own set of nicknames for her, having given her that one years ago for her sweet nature and quaking temper.

"Hi." A wan smile crossed her lips.

"How are you, love?" I kissed her cheek before sitting down.

"I'm okay. Better now that you're here."

"I need you to forgive me, Kennedy. I haven't meant to neglect you. Just all these discoveries about Skylar have me so confused," I admitted.

"Like what?"

"Aside from the money and bonds, he'd been researching some things and it doesn't seem like he'd ever gotten any concrete answers. Now I am picking up where he left off. I still don't know very much, but I promise to fill you in as soon as I know something for sure or at least something that makes sense."

Kennedy nodded.

I couldn't have been more surprised that she hadn't argued with me about telling her right then, but I thought she may have been more worried about Bryant. She knew I'd would come around, at some point.

"You said Bryant's been asking you questions about me, what kind of questions?" I asked.

She sighed.

"Questions about you and about Skylar. Whether you kept secrets from each other..." Her expression changed, contorting her face and I tried to imagine what her thoughts were. "He also asked me something about some money..."

My stomach sank and I noticed a far off look in her eyes.

"Did you tell him about the money or the safe box?" I closed my eyes as I waited for her answer.

"No, no. I didn't think you wanted anyone to know." She stared at the napkin in her hands, tearing it into small pieces.

I resumed breathing, willing myself not to sigh aloud.

"Yeah, no, you're right. I don't want anybody to know. Why do you think he's asking so many questions all of a sudden?"

"I don't know, it's weird."

What would make Bryant ask about—? I didn't complete that thought because it'd been cut off by another: *He knows!* Oh, my God! If he knew about the investments, then he must have known about the returns. This awareness brought on my own line of questions making me wonder how much Bryant knew. My mind flashed to the pictures of Bryant from the file. He couldn't have known about them but maybe he did. The possibilities put new fear in my heart, but I didn't want to alarm Kennedy. I needed a more concrete foundation before revealing too much to her. She'd hate me for keeping such a huge secret, but I didn't feel as if I had much choice. Kennedy, more apt to make rash decisions, would fight against this rip current without a second thought but the situation required more of a leveled head than panic.

I tried to be smooth and changed the subject, hoping to relax us both, and told her about my hike with Seth. She, knowing me better than anyone, became hysterical with laughter, picturing me stumbling to my knees every third step, while Seth walked with a smooth and agile gait. We drank a couple of bottles of sake while we talked and laughed, holding up the table long enough for the wait staff to change shifts. It felt like we hadn't talked in the longest time.

I never made it to the office, instead, I went in early the next morning, having slacked off, thanks to all the detective work I'd been doing. Making a pretty big dent in my workload before noon kept me from canceling with Santiago and I arrived at the loft a few minutes ahead of schedule. Pulling up through the gate, I parked next to his truck and trotted up the stairs.

"Hello?" I called out.

"Sí. Uh, yeah!" Santiago answered from somewhere inside.

"It's Echo, where are you?"

"I'm aware of that." *Wise guy,* I thought. "I'm in the master."

Glancing around as I walked through the loft, I noticed lots of little things he'd completed. Impressive.

"Hi." I said to his legs, stemming from beneath bathroom countertop.

"Hey there," he said around a grunt. "Just one second."

"Sure."

"Ready?"

I didn't think he'd meant a literal second.

"Umm-hmm."

He pulled himself from under the sink, dusting off his jeans as he stood. I took a step back.

"Oh, wait." He took hold of me, his hand a fiery cuff around my forearm.

I looked down at his hand where my skin smoldered beneath it. He kept talking as though he hadn't even realized he'd grabbed me. He didn't seem aware at all.

"There is toilet number one."

He gestured to the installed toilet in the corner of the bathroom with his free hand.

"You can try it out if you like. I'll be a gentleman and leave you two alone," he taunted with a smile.

Somewhere between one taunt and another, laughter filled the unfinished room. A delayed sense of recognition came over me; the laughter had been mine. His humor and my amusement surprised me. He showed me the other two toilets, again offering me alone time which I declined around giggles and smiles.

"Have you had lunch yet?" he asked.

"No, not yet."

"Do you want to grab a bite before we go shopping? I started working this morning and forgot to eat breakfast."

"Sure. I don't see a problem with that. I mean, a girl's gotta eat!"

He smiled. We walked out to his truck and he held the door open for me.

"Hey, how's your leg?"

"No gangrene and it hasn't fallen off, so I suppose

it's okay." I smiled.

"You must have had all your shots!"

A smile formed around his eyes. I shot him an I-can't-believe-you-just-said-that look, which turned his smile into a chortle.

"I haven't been to this place in years," I said of *In-N-Out Burger,* when he parked in front of the building. "Skylar was so health conscious..." I trailed off, never finishing the sentence, but it wasn't because of sadness though I couldn't decipher what I felt.

"I figured it had been a while since you had a five-star dining experience." I threw my left hand into his chest. We chuckled as he shrank away.

Santiago ordered for the both of us, never bothering to ask me what I'd prefer. The smells made me hungrier. We talked, filling the space of time between ordering and eating. He'd ordered us both a double-double, fries, and vanilla shakes. I would have liked strawberry, but I wasn't going to complain.

Before taking the first fry to his mouth, Santiago bowed his head over the meal and took hold of my hand. For at least the third time that day, he'd confounded me. The unexpected act again, left me speechless. He recited a short prayer, blessing our food, let go of my hand, and dug in. My palm burned from his touch. Following his lead, I lifted the huge burger to my mouth and took the largest bite I could manage.

"Mmm!" The sound came from the base of my throat, though I hadn't intended to make it aloud.

I'd closed my eyes, so I couldn't see Santiago's reaction but I'd hoped he wasn't staring at me as though I were some oddity the way Seth had. After swallowing the first sumptuous bite, I opened my eyes.

"Good, isn't it?" Santiago asked, even before my eyes had focused.

"Oh, my gosh!"

I shoved another french fry into my already full mouth. My manners had gone on an impromptu vacation but I didn't *feel* ill-mannered, strange, or gluttonous, even if I were all of those things.

"I love a woman that's not afraid to eat..." A look of admiration glossed his eyes. "Or get her hands dirty."

"Then you must love me!" I shot back, unmindful about what I should or shouldn't have said, at least not in that moment.

After stuffing our faces, I had no room for the shake, but I brought it with me anyway, refusing to throw it away despite being full.

"You won't get your fingers cut off for throwing that away, you know, and no one will starve if you do." He grinned.

"I know, but I want it. It's against the laws of my

nature to throw away sweets."

"Suit yourself." He shrugged.

I didn't pay much attention to the direction he drove for the chatter we'd engaged in. When I, at last, looked out the window, I noticed we were far from the home improvement store I thought we were going to.

"Where are we going? Isn't the store in the other direction?"

"I'm taking you somewhere different. That other place is fine for your tush, but this place has a much better selection of basins and tubs. You'll love it, I promise. Just wait and see."

He spoke with such confidence, as though he'd known me for years; as if he'd invested countless hours learning my most favorable and unfavorable things. How could he speak with such certainty about someone he didn't know?

We pulled up to what looked like a spruced up junkyard, a beautiful disarray. I'd been so busy gawking, I hadn't noticed Santiago standing in the door with an extended hand.

"Ahem." I snapped my head in his direction. "I told you you'd love it and we haven't even walked inside yet." He wore a self-assured smile.

The gawking continued when I walked in. The place, with its eclectic decor, incorporated sinks like works of art. Shimmering tiles lined the walls from ceiling to floor. Basin after basin in various hues, textures, and materials covered square inch after square inch. He'd been correct in his judgment...I *did* love the place but choosing one sink among the myriad of choices wouldn't be easy.

"You get to pick three you know," he said as though my thoughts had been floating tangibly in the air.

"I do, don't I?"

I bounded through the store with new enthusiasm, Santiago right on my heels. I deliberated and agonized over which would look good where. As the last time, Santiago insisted on making his opinion known, not that I'd asked.

"Would you like some help?" a salesman asked us as I looked from one sink to the other.

"I'm just waiting for the lady to make up her mind," Santiago sighed. "She won't listen to me."

"Women," the man replied in a conspiratorial voice. "My wife won't listen to a word I say either."

I turned around to object to the insinuation, but Santiago spoke before I did.

"That one is going to clash with the fixtures you chose." He ignored the comment the salesman had made and pointed at the sink I'd been mulling over. "Not to mention the tile in the shower."

"But I like it."

We went back and forth for so long the salesman backed away without acknowledgement from either of us. By the time we were done squabbling, Santiago had become flustered because he'd had to persuade me to change my mind and I'd grown annoyed because he'd actually done it.

The sales guy had enough of us both but deciding which tubs to get had been a lot less tumultuous.

Making our way back outside, the breezes blew cool air thanks to the sinking sun. It felt as if we'd spent the entire day inside that store. I consulted my watch and the time startled me being almost seven p.m. Wow, who knew choosing bath furniture could be so time consuming. Tension swirled around us and frustration filled the cab of the truck. On a heaving sigh, Santiago mumbled something in Spanish, heightening my annoyance.

"What?" I yelled. "What!"

"You're insufferable, that's what!"

"Me? What about you?" I threw a hand up, gesturing to him.

"What about me? I'm not the one who takes eight weeks to pick out a damned sink! You won't listen to anyone—"

"Not anyone, just not you!" I spat.

I wanted out of his ratty truck, to get away from his crappy attitude. Again, he rambled in Spanish which, I'm sure, he knew how irritating that was.

"Oh, I doubt, Ms. Wells, if I'm the only one that you turn a deaf ear to."

"Maybe if you spoke in English, I'd at least pretend to listen."

We were so busy carrying on that neither of us saw the red light until we were a third of the way through it.

"Santi—!"

"Shit!" He looked at the light, gripping the steering wheel as he looked left and right.

We swerved and then took a hard turn. I felt one side of the truck lift off the ground, sliding me across the seat towards Santiago. The tires screeched and we hit a large bump, coming to an abrupt halt, pitching me forward.

Someone screamed and I heard glass shatter along with other loud sounds. With my face in my wet hands, I crouched into a ball, afraid to look. I heard someone sobbing and thought for a moment that it might have been Santiago but somehow realized it wasn't. My knees felt warm and moist. Oh, God I was bleeding! I felt the wetness in my palms and panic began to rise, but still too afraid to look, I sat there near motionless.

"Mi vida. Are you okay? Por favor, stop crying."

The sobbing had gotten louder. I heard doors closing, sirens blaring and crying that verged on screaming.

"Silencio, mi querida. I've got you. Esta bien."

The whispers sounded close to my ear while a breeze made the blood which saturated me turn cool.

"No!" I screamed, flinching as someone reached for me. "No! Leave me, leave me here! I don't want to leave him alone!"

I hadn't opened my eyes but still, I tried to fight the person who'd put their hand on my back, slapping them away.

"No! Stop it! My baby!"

He wouldn't listen to my screams, so I forced my eyes open despite being afraid of what I'd see. The sobbing had stopped, sirens quieted and nearby I heard a Spanish lullaby. I couldn't understand the words, but it had a drug-like effect on me. My focus began to sharpen, but I closed my eyes against the vision.

Gentle rocking and the smell of fresh cut cucumbers and mint lulled me. Curiosity willed me to open my eyes and my senses urged me to feel. When I looked at my knees, I learned the moisture I'd felt had not been blood but tears, evident by my damp face and eyelashes. Someone brushed away an escaped tear from my cheek.

A lullaby sang in one ear and the beat of a rapid heart drummed in the other. A car horn blared as it sped by, making me jump. His arms pulled me closer and I hugged myself, concluding that the tortured sobs had come from me.

Lifting my eyes, I saw parts of Santiago. I hadn't realized he'd been the one holding me but in an instant, the picture completed itself. Santiago sat at the curb with me in his arms singing a lullaby into my ear and rocking me like a newborn babe. The cucumber and mint aroma wafted from his neck and the fierce, drumming heartbeat I'd been listening to wasn't mine but his.

"Lo siento. I'm so sorry. I'd never hurt you." he said and then continued singing.

I took a deep breath of him and wrapped my arms around his neck, finding comfort in his embrace. Santiago had removed his shirt and used to dry my face and hands. We sat there for a while longer, then he lifted us from the curb and placed me back into the truck's cab. He climbed in on the other side and pulled me across the seat into the vacant space under his arm. I felt a measure of safety there, an inexplicable refuge. He kept his eyes trained on the road while using his free arm to drive, revealing a tattoo which decorated his limb from shoulder to wrist in a dark swirling pattern. I burrowed close to him, keeping my eyes closed, listening as he sang his lullaby.

When we pulled to a soft stop, I opened my eyes expecting to be parked next to my truck back at the loft. Instead, he had brought us to a small restaurant which looked more like someone's house. He all but carried me inside and led us to a little booth away from all the other tables.

I wasn't surprised when Santiago ordered for both

of us again, something I'd already grown accustomed to. He'd ordered a bottle of wine as well, sliding a half-full glass across to me. I took a long sip, well, more like a gulp, enjoying the fruity flavor and the effects of the wine's potency. By the third glass, I'd relaxed but more tears flowed, however, this time they were generated by laughter. We shuffled out of the eatery arm in arm, trailing giggles and mirth in our wake. The rest of the night floated by in a happy haze.

Seven

 awoke to the smell of cappuccino. Peeling my eyes open, I peered through my veil of hair. Flipping it behind me, I looked around at all my things unable to remember how I'd gotten home or in my bed. I still had on all my clothes even though I lay tucked under the covers which seemed to be happening more often. On my bedside table sat a breakfast tray with a steaming cup of cappuccino, a small white box tied with a bow, two aspirin, and a note. I noticed the box from a bakery down the street, an assortment of baked goods inside. I smiled and picked up the note. It read:

Breakfast of champions, now eat up and get to work! I'll see you later.

Santiago

I lay back on the pillows, my smile widening until it faded as I pondered last night. Had he spent the night? I looked over at Skylar's side of the bed and sure enough, I saw a large indentation on the surface of the comforter. I rolled over and the cool smell of cucumbers had permeated the fibers of the pillow case. I may not have remembered everything that happened last night but I remembered one thing—his scent. He had slept here and on top of the covers from the looks of it. I wasn't sure how I felt about that.

Sitting up cross-legged in the bed, I popped the aspirin into my mouth and swallowed them without water. Then I took a bite of one of the sweet treats from the box. After a few sips of cappuccino, I crawled out of bed. *Wait, where's my car?* I wondered. If he'd driven me home, that meant I'd have to take a cab to pick up my truck. I walked out into the living room to look for my phone to call him but spotted my keys and purse on the counter. How did he—? Did he drive my car here? Why couldn't I remember the exchange, and how did he get home? I searched my purse for my phone, but it wasn't there. I scanned the room for it but my gaze locked on the pile of papers I hadn't even allowed Kennedy to see.

"Dammit!" I said aloud.

There they were in plain sight. I wondered if he'd seen them. Of course he had, you can't miss them sitting right here. I tried hard to recall last night, but all that came to mind was good wine and lots of laughs. Santiago proved to be great company when he wasn't cursing me in a foreign language. I started to smile, but stopped myself; this wasn't a laughing matter. A stranger knowing the details of such sensitive information, not to mention all the unresolved matters which included, well, most of it.

I stalked back to my room, angry with myself for being so careless. Looking for my phone, my eyes trailed a path back to the night stand where my phone sat beside the box of goodies, plugged into its charger. I picked it up, snatching the wire, intending to call Santiago, but I didn't know what to say.

"Hey, did you see those conspiracy files on my kitchen counter? Can you pretend you didn't?" The questions sounded even more stupid aloud than they did in my head.

I put the phone down, not knowing what to do. I read his note again, written in his muddled penmanship. 'I'll see you later' it said. I must have agreed to meet him again but I, for sure, needed to go to work and get some things done, for a change.

After getting dressed, I went back into the living room, grabbed my purse and keys and headed for the door. I took a quick look back and turned to the door but something gave me pause. One of the pictures on the table caught my eye. Walking over, I slid the photo on top to the side, gaping at the face revealed underneath. I knew something had been familiar about that face. My memory flashed to the fuzzy black and white photo from the old newspaper article I'd found in the library. I looked again.

In my head, the images were side by side.

"Holy..."

Ali. The man in the picture was Jahi Ali. In the photo he stood next to Bryant and as I flipped through, I saw him in almost every picture with Bryant somewhere nearby; talking to him, standing behind him, taking a brief case from him. The connections brightened, but the lines blurred. What had Bryant been up to? What had he done and why would he involve himself with such a creep? I stood there staring at the pictures in wonderment. I could speculate for hours. I needed to get back to the library to see what else I could find but I knew I wouldn't make it today, too much work to do.

I rushed out the door, stuffing the disheveled papers into my bag and heading to my truck. I went down to the garage to my assigned space, but it wasn't there. My eyes bulged, and I spun in a circle, as if dizzying myself would make my car appear where it had not been before. Instead, the dizzy spell brought me to a more logical thought: Santiago. He must have driven my car here and taken a cab home. He wouldn't have known where to park it. Goodness, it could be anywhere. I went to the lobby, happy to see Trevor there.

"Hi, Trevor. My truck is—"

"It's right out front." He didn't bother letting me finish. "This morning, a Mr. Ruiz told me he'd parked it there for you...said he was a friend of yours. Is everything okay, he isn't lying is he?"

Trevor had that speculative look in his eyes again. Trevor most often remained very calm and quiet but, as of late, he appeared to be a little on edge.

"No, it's okay. He's fine. Thanks."

I dashed out the glass doors before he could inquire any further. When I got into the truck, I noticed an ornament hanging from my rearview mirror. It wasn't anything I'd purchased, that's for sure. A note hung from a string along with a small cut of near translucent tile. I recognized it from the store Santiago had taken me to remembering how I'd raved about the beauty of the iridescent tile. Smiling, I read the short note:

Just thought I'd return the favor: I got to spend the night with a beauty, thought you might want to spend the day with one.

Santiago

So the sourpuss had a softer side. What an unexpected gesture. It made me contemplate what had happened last night, what I might have said. I would guess I'd said a lot or too much, maybe both. Sighing at my inability to recall, I pulled away from the curb and headed to my office. This would be the reason I stayed away from alcohol. I hated the uncertainty.

A slew of messages waited for me at my desk.

Flipping through them, I saw that most were from vendors and two were from Seth. I'd have to call him later. Organizing my messages from most important to least important, Seth ended up near the bottom of the pile. I reassured myself that I'd call him before the end of the day, disregarding the order of importance in my mind. I went to work, calling one vendor after another, making appointments, setting dates, and smoothing out details. By three o'clock, I had made real progress and called Kennedy to check-in.

We were still talking when my receptionist, Jessica, popped her head into my office. Her brown hair fell like curtain from her head, the edges blunt and in a perfect, symmetrical line. Her eyes were wide on a regular day among her petite features, but stood even wider as she looked at me. She had a smug grin on her face, as if she were privy to a secret I had not yet heard and a dreamy expression crinkled the lines of her face.

"Echo—I mean, Ms. Wells?" she paused.

"Yes?" I pulled the phone away from my mouth.

"You have a visitor." She stepped to the side before I could ask any more questions.

A moment later someone else stood in my doorway. I didn't realize I'd smiled until I felt the gentle tensing in my cheeks. He returned my smile with a brilliant reflection of his own. Straight, white teeth shone, surrounded by copious, blush-tinted lips. Tender looking lips, like a ripened, juice-filled fruit. That face had housed many smiles and birthed much laughter, that I had been a witness to. I couldn't stop staring at the man's lips. It seemed as if I hadn't seen them until this moment and they had never looked so good.

"Well, well, well. Look who made it back to this side of sobriety," Santiago's voice, spiked with sarcasm, pulled my eyes upwards, to his face.

"Shh!" I hoped no one else had heard his comment and by "no one," I meant, Jessica.

She'd be sure to tell every associate within earshot about the pony-tailed stranger Ms. Wells had gotten drunk with.

He strolled through the door, his gait casual, almost arrogant. That explained Jessica's starry eyes when she'd said I had a visitor. He didn't look like the average client, and he, for certain, didn't behave like one. Even his walk defied that assumption. I wanted to close the door, keep a barrier between us and everyone else, but I thought that might make matters worse, draw more attention to present company.

"What are you doing here?" I stood up and while raising my body from the chair, I lowered the phone to the hook without saying goodbye to Kennedy.

"We have a lunch date. Come on." The statement sounded more like a demand than a reminder.

Date? Like a date, date? I giggled, thinking about Kennedy, Skylar, and Bryant and our inside joke. Maybe it does mean something different when you said it twice. It did to me right now. I returned my attention to him, noticing his scowl. At first, I couldn't understand why; I hadn't said anything. How could he manage such a radiant smile and menacing frown on the same face without any side effects? He looked like two different people, then it occurred to me, that he may have thought I'd laughed at him. I didn't know how to recover without insulting him further.

"I'm sorry. I wasn't laughing at you," I gathered my belongings. "I just thought of something. Are you ready?" It sounded more like a lie than the truth.

"Yes." he answered in a brusque tone.

As we walked toward the exit together, Jessica couldn't even pretend to contain herself. Maybe it wasn't the best idea to leave with him where she could see, but it was too late to worry about it. By the time we got to the lobby, his face had softened. We walked outside into the sunshine, and to my right, a gleam of green caught my attention.

In front of the building, a half-moon driveway paved a path from the parking lot to the entrance. On either side, an awning covered the walkway and parked on that walkway, in true rebel fashion, I saw a sparkling, emerald green motorcycle. How I'd recognized this motorcycle from so many months ago, I'll never know, but the picture resurrected itself upon sight. I imagined the green machine speeding by me on the 101 all over again. My memory flashed the scene in my head and I shook off the memory.

"Are you okay?" Santiago turned to me. "You can't be cold; it's ninety degrees out."

"It's just that bike..." I pointed and he followed my finger with his eyes. "I recognize it. That idiot cut me off on the freeway a while back, scared the crap out of me. Jerk!"

"Do you mind if we take your car because I rode my bike today?" He'd asked, as if I'd said nothing at all.

A helmet materialized in his left hand. My mouth fell open and I questioned how I hadn't seen it before. I'd been so dazzled by his smile, I hadn't noticed much else. He shook the helmet in his hand, taunting me.

"Unless you want to go for a ride?" he teased.

My expression remained frozen in place. With a single finger, he lifted my gaping jaw to meet my upper lip.

"That's yours? That was you!"

He smiled.

"Not that I remember, but what makes you so sure it was me? Do you know how many bikers there are in California?"

"No, but I know *that* motorcycle!"

He laughed and the rich sound distracted me. He had a hearty laugh that seemed to stem from somewhere deep inside his chest. I didn't know whether to be annoyed, amused, or appalled. I let the mixture bounce around my insides like a ping pong ball.

"Where's your car?"

Why did he keep doing that, pretending I hadn't said anything? Without a word, I moved forward, hearing his chuckles echo behind me. He continued to snicker as he opened my door. I rolled my eyes and got in. A grin found its way to my face when I gazed at the tile hanging from my rearview mirror, swinging in the breeze.

"I take it you like your trinket." He pointed to the tile. "You must have stared at that tile for twenty minutes... and you kept touching it.

I hadn't been aware he'd paid such close attention to me.

"It's beautiful." I marveled at the way the sun shone on it.

"I knew you'd like it," he gloated. "Well, I'm hungry, what are you in the mood for?"

I took him to one of my favorite bistros and since we were between lunch and dinner, the place was pretty quiet. I ran off at the mouth again; it appeared I'd been having trouble filtering my words.

"So you said Kennedy doesn't know about Bryant's

dealings, but she knows about the money. Are you going to tell her? Don't you think she should know?" he asked.

His question proved that he *did* know about the situation with Skylar and Bryant and not because he'd read through my files, but because I'd told him. I couldn't cover up, sugar coat, or dismiss it. I couldn't take back what he knew, but that didn't make me any less apprehensive about continuing to reveal these secrets. On the other hand, I felt a great sense of relief in being to talk to someone. I assumed he knew everything I did, considering I'd told him about the money too. I exhaled; unable to believe how much I had told this man I knew little about.

A light in the corner of my mind began shining light on tidbits of last night and conversations we'd had. Santiago's tongue had loosened as well, and he'd revealed things, which gave me a clearer picture of him.

Born in Puerto Rico, he'd lived there until he turned sixteen. He'd been the youngest of three and the only boy until losing one of his sisters to leukemia at a young age. The family relocated to New Mexico, where he stayed until his early twenties, attended college and gotten his degree. I couldn't remember where he'd gone to college or what he'd gotten his degree in. Architecture, maybe? It couldn't be. He wouldn't be just some contractor if he were sitting on a degree like that. His parents had moved back to Puerto Rico not long after he'd turned twenty-three, but he refused to return with them, straining their relationship. He'd married at twenty-five to a woman his parents hadn't approved of, causing more tension between them. He couldn't understand their dislike for his bride until after she'd given birth to their daughter, Helena. His parents' aversion would define itself within the first few months of Helena's life.

Cristina, his now ex-wife, became a very different woman, according to Santiago. He said she'd become demanding and money, he'd discovered, had been her true love. Santiago had traded a job he'd loved for a job he'd hated to make Cristina happy and to ensure that neither she nor Cristina wanted for anything and she had not worked a day since they'd married, but it wasn't enough. Just after Helena's first birthday, Cristina filed for a divorce, claiming Santiago had been vacant and worked too many hours, leaving her to care for a newborn alone. Helena gave her an excuse to demand even more money from him.

Cristina had come from a poor town in Colombia, so marrying Santiago had been a dream, but divorcing him and still getting his money was a fantasy. The courts granted her alimony and child support and with that she fled back to Colombia to flaunt her new wealth, ignoring Santiago's attempts to see Helena. Being out of the country made it easier for her to avoid him and harder for him to have a hand in raising his daughter. He'd told me he hadn't seen her in two years.

I couldn't understand how he wasn't fighting for her. If I'd had a chance to get back the baby I'd lost—even to death—there would be no stopping me. A chill ran the length of my spine and I heard laughter resonate in my ears and then die down, replaced by Santiago's words. Though the restaurant had been next to empty, we still spoke in hushed voices.

"What's the matter?" he asked.

"Nothing, just thinking. What did you ask me?"

"I asked you about Kennedy and Bryant, what are you going to do? Are you going to tell her?"

"I want some more information first. I want to, at least, be able to explain what went on and what's happening now."

Although I couldn't find the logic in telling Santiago...well, everything, it didn't feel wrong nor did it feel like a mistake. It felt...normal to talk to him.

"That makes sense, but you don't think she's in danger, do you?"

"No. Bryant isn't violent. He barely hits a tennis ball hard enough to hurt it," I giggled. "Besides, I think Kennedy could take him. She's no lightweight."

He laughed aloud, an infectious laugh, making my smile widen. We continued to talk in low timbres and by the end of it, I'd divulged the entire, sordid mess. He had some interesting perspectives and connected some dots that I had not. Unbeknownst to him, this frightened me more with every clue and placed piece.

"So the company, *Finge Inc*..." I said.

"Wait, what?" He leaned closer. "The name of the

company, say it again."

"Finge."

"Finge," he repeated.

"Yes."

"Finge is Spanish for fake or false."

"What?"

"It means fake en español."

Sly little devils had given the company a name that stated its intent, and no one had been the wiser. Even Santiago had not caught on right away, and his native language is Spanish.

"I can't believe it!" I said.

"It's like hiding in plain sight. It's a bold move, but it worked."

"No kidding. Hmm..."

"What?"

"I read an article on Ali, and he had what they called a 'ghost company' which they'd set up to scam people out of their money. This sounds like the same thing. It's called, uh, something like Rigatoni."

He laughed and I realized that I'd just named a type of pasta. I giggled too, shaking my head in mock shame. I dug around in my purse and found where I had written the name down.

"Raggiro," I corrected. His smile faded. I could almost see the wheels spinning in his head. "What?"

He chanted under his breath, but I couldn't make out his words.

"Tell me," I demanded.

"Raggiro is Italian," he took a long pause.

"And..." I urged him to continue.

"It also means fake."

"Are you kidding me? How do you know?"

"I worked in Italy for a while...Rome. I helped refurbish some residential homes for an American businessman. He'd bought a lot of them for—"

"So this guy is setting up phantom companies and businesses over and over again just to con people out of their hard-earned money?" I'd phrased my observation as a question, although I wasn't asking.

"That's what it sounds like."

"Okay, the article I read said that he'd been jailed for it once before. How is it he's getting away with it again?"

"Well, it's not that hard. Anybody can start a business of any sort without much trouble. Lots of business is conducted online, eliminating the need to have a building or property or anything concrete. It's easier now than ever, all you need is an address," he explained.

I thought of the pictures of Ali with Bryant and wondered how deep his involvement went and how much he knew about this guy. I wondered if he'd been as oblivious as Skylar.

"We need to go," I said.

"Why? What's wrong?"

"I need to show you something, but not here."

So much made sense but I couldn't be certain of where the enlightenment had come from. I needed him. I needed his fresh eyes and unbiased thinking. Santiago paid the bill, cramming some folded bills into the waitress' hand and we scurried out the door. I'd forgotten about his motorcycle and the time because it was now six-thirty p.m. It didn't make sense to go to my closed office, but I had loaded my attaché with event details and a to-do list to work on after hours.

I wanted to show Santiago the article from the library, but it had already closed for the day. Either way, I wanted to review these pages with a sober mind, now that things were making more sense.

We drove back to my office to get his bike and he tailed me back to my place. I pulled into my assigned parking spot and he angled his bike behind my Volvo, taking up the last bit of space between the lines. I stole glances at him through my side view mirror. He had on a white tank top, showcasing his muscled arms as he stretched to reach the handlebars. A pair of khaki cargo shorts, and low profile sneakers allowed me to see his legs for the first time. I almost laughed at their girth, or lack of. His legs were small, but he had prominent calves. He had taken off his helmet and sunglasses, but left on his khaki hat, which he wore backwards and made his way to my door. I hoped he hadn't seen me staring, because I'd surpassed glancing at him and moved into full-on ogling.

I feigned busyness by shuffling miscellaneous items from the console to the seat and back again. He'd walked up to my window before my second rotation. He just stood there with a mischievous grin lining one side of his face. His eyes, a sweet, tantalizing shade of warm caramel were wide as he gazed at me through the glass. His skin, the color of toasted butterscotch, glistened with sweat. *Why is he just standing there?* I thought. He had a questioning look on his face and my eyebrows scrunched together in return. He pointed downward, and followed his finger with my eyes. I felt ditzy and laughed at myself while pressing the button to unlock the doors.

His grin had transformed, now covering his entire face. I stepped out of the car and we strolled upstairs to my unit. Taking out my keys, I aimed for the lock but before I'd inserted my key the door pushed open. I knew I'd locked it, so I didn't understand how door hadn't just been unlocked but ajar. Santiago gave me a quizzical look. He stepped in front of me and pushed the door open wide, his hand sliding across the surface. I gasped. My place was in shambles. Paper and trash littered the floor, drawers and cabinets stood open. I went to take a step forward, but Santiago extended his strong arm across my chest like a lift gate in a parking garage. He motioned for me to be quiet and stay put.

From his side, he pulled out a gun. My eyes almost jumped out of their sockets and pain tugged at the nerves behind them. I watched after him, nervous and scared. He turned around to me, putting his thumb to his ear and his pinky to his mouth.

"Call the police," he mouthed.

I nodded dumbly, but didn't move right away. A moment later, without taking my eyes from his back, I my phone dug out of my bag and dialed 911.

"There's been a break-in at my home," I heard myself say.

I hadn't listened to the operator's instructions or questions but recited my address and hung up while sounds were still coming from the other end of the line. I peered after Santiago. I couldn't hear his footsteps but since I hadn't heard any gunshots either, I didn't panic—much. By the time I'd blinked again, he had returned to my line of sight and had also put away his gun. He looked more relaxed as he walked up to me and put an arm around my waist, a silent assurance.

"Check to see if anything's missing, okay? That way

when the police get here you can let them know."

"Okay," I agreed, on a tiny breath.

As I walked through, scanning with my eyes and memory, Santiago remained close, never moving his arm from around me. I could not have been more grateful for his presence, his comfort, and silent fortitude. The door to the former nursery stood wide open exposing the load of boxes inside. Each one had sat sealed for months, but now they were spread all over the room having been opened with careless, reckless abandon. Baby clothes, bottles, and accessories had been scattered everywhere. Seeing all the gifts in plain sight tugged at my heart, but my thoughts drifted from my unborn child to Helena, something I couldn't define nor explain. Santiago pulled me closer to his side. We heard a knock on the front door, still ajar, and turned around.

"Mr. and Mrs. Wells?" Two cops stood in the doorway with Trevor between them.

I knew it had been one of the officers who'd spoken, assuming Santiago to be "Mr. Wells." I almost laughed but neither Santiago nor I spoke. I suppose he'd wait for me to correct them but I never did. However, Trevor whispered into both their ears, receiving dual nods in return. I saw the alarm in Trevor's eyes, and his shoulders were rigid. They didn't allow him to come in, but he watched every move they made from his post at the door. I thought he would've returned to the lobby before they were done, after all, we had an entire building that needed surveillance, even more now.

The cops swept the place and interviewed Santiago, myself, and Trevor since he wouldn't leave. They'd said the entry hadn't been forced and asked who else may have had keys. I had one answer: Kennedy. They'd questioned me about her too. They'd asked me, well, us a host of questions which, on any other day, would seem asinine. Today, however, in light of everything that had been unveiled, the line of questioning sounded logical.

I'd never thought answering questions could be so exhausting. Once everyone had left, I plopped down onto the couch with an exasperated sigh. Santiago had begun cleaning, despite my objections.

"Try to relax." He brought me a blanket, pillow, and cup of hot tea.

I hadn't even heard the kettle or microwave. I took his offerings and lay there listening to his movement around the condo. I couldn't decide which was stranger, Santiago cleaning my place or the fact that I was comfortable with it. After a while, he came to sit next to me on the couch.

"How are you?" He spoke just above a whisper, draping his arm around my shoulders.

"I'm okay. I'm really glad you're here. I don't know how well I would've handled this otherwise."

My gaze fell on the closed door of the tousled, incomplete nursery. He'd been intuitive enough to pull the door shut, shielding my eyes from the mess. Also, cutting off latent thoughts of a lost child. I felt his eyes on me, but I dared not look, afraid of what my soul might see in his eyes or what his might see in mine.

"Do you think Ali was behind this, because I sure do?" he half asked.

"I'm certain of it. I bet he'd thought he'd find the money here. There have been messages saying they knew about the box and the money. I'm sure they thought I'd hidden it in the condo."

"So, it's not here? They didn't get it?"

"No, when they said they knew about it, the same day I put it in a safety deposit box at a bank near the loft," I admitted.

"Smart girl."

Speaking about this in private made me think of why he'd come to my house in the first place. I sprang up from the couch, leaving him with a confused expression. He didn't ask any questions. I sat down next to him a moment later, closer than before, and pulled the files from my case, relieved that I'd taken them with me. He waited, not saying a word, surprising me again. He didn't impress me as patient at all. I handed him the pictures that included Bryant.

"Who's this with Bryant?" he asked.

"I'm almost positive it's Ali, the guy who started

this whole mess. I wanted to take you to the library to show you the article I'd read."

"We can go first thing in the morning."

"Okay."

I told him about the private investigator and what I'd found out. Chances of the information being redundant were high, considering I had blabbed my mouth the night before. Just because I hadn't remembered, didn't mean he hadn't.

Eight

We talked until sleep overcame us, wading through subjects like swimmers. When I awoke, ensconced in his embrace, I noticed he'd shifted me to the inside seam of the couch, where we'd fallen victim to exhaustion. I'd buried my face in the crook of his neck and inhaled the sultry scent of him. How he'd managed to always smell so pleasant even when he'd been sweaty, I'll never figure. His soft snore sounded almost melodic. No wonder I'd been so drowsy. I shifted my eyes, trying to determine how I could get out of his hold but not before deciding to lay there for a few more minutes.

I looked up at him, feeling his breath against my forehead in timed intervals. I felt his body with every limb of mine. We were so close that we had entwined our legs while we'd slept. We lay there like lovers. A comfort accumulated by many nights and moments like these but the man was a stranger to me. I could imagine what the scene would seem to an onlooker. The sentiment, the quiet grin, the head cocked to the side and soft eyes as though watching a sleeping child. A precious sight worthy of remembrance. I did feel quite comfortable, inertia settling into my muscles. I squirmed and he drew me into him. I hadn't thought we could get much closer on the small sofa but I'd been wrong.

I inched downward little by little, still reluctant to move. Despite his unconscious efforts to keep me there, I freed myself, although it felt more like abandonment. I slithered to the end of the couch, skimming past his legs which hung over the arm of the sofa, careful not to touch them. My feet dangled and I pushed myself up with more force than needed. My upper body soared up and over the edge. Before I could get my footing, I hit the floor, silencing the thud I would've made if I hadn't caught myself on my fingertips. He shifted positions. I heard the friction of his clothes against the chair's fabric. Peeking up over couch, relived I hadn't woken him, I tiptoed towards my room, listening as his rhythmic breathing continued. Two steps before I'd made it there, I heard two quick raps on the door and the key in the lock.

"Shoot!" I almost swore but caught myself.

I tracked my bare feet across the room to the door with record speed—at least for me. I heard the lock slide to the side and the door fell open. Before Kennedy had completed an intake of breath, I clamped my hand over her mouth. Her eyes went wide as she reached up to remove it.

"Shh!" I mouthed, pointing to the sofa.

I couldn't hide Santiago. Her expression went from confused, to mischievous, to elated. She kicked off her heels at the door and closed it without making a sound. I dragged her by the arm into my bathroom and shut the door.

"What is the sexy salvager doing here? And on your couch no less! Did you sleep with him? How was it? This place is a wreck and I see you never made it to the bed. Dish!" Her eyes beamed.

"No, I didn't sleep with him! Well, sort of... technically. Nothing happened. We fell asleep on the couch." I whispered; though I didn't know why because she wasn't even trying to be quiet.

"So you *did* sleep with him!" A sly grin stretched across her face.

"Shut up!" I slapped her on the shoulder.

"So are you two dating now? What happened to Chef Hottie?"

"Shit!" I couldn't catch myself that time. "I was supposed to call him yesterday. Crap! I don't know what's going on with us. He wants to take me hiking again." I grimaced. Kennedy burst into laughter. Well, guffaw is better word.

"Shh!" I giggled.

"No wonder you haven't called the guy. I wouldn't either. So you've blown him off to take up residence with the Bilingual Builder, have you?" *Where did she come up with these names?*

"No, we've been shopping for the loft."

"And that requires a sleepover? Hell, if I weren't a married woman, I'd buy my own damned loft just for the candy it comes with!" We laughed, but she switched gears in an instant. "You do realize we have an event today, don't you?"

"I do now." With all that had happened, I'd pretty much forgotten. "Can I meet you at the Coffee Bean in an hour—the one near your office?" I looked toward the closed door. "Hour and a half?"

"Need a morning romp in the sack before getting to your day job, do ya?" Leave it to Kennedy to turn everything dirty.

"I wish."

"I knew it!" She pointed at me.

I'd really just said that out loud. There's no denying I had and Kennedy would not let me forget.

"Kidding! I'm kidding!"

"The hell you are. I knew this would turn into something the moment you met him. You laid eyes on him and I disappeared."

"Yes, you did. You went out and sat in the car for forty-five minutes."

"No, I sat in the car for *fifteen* minutes. The two of you ignored me, so I left. Not that I needed you to, but you didn't even introduce me! I stood next to you talking and asking questions and neither of you acknowledged that I was even there. I'm surprised you didn't jump each other on sight."

I thought back to that day and how quiet she'd been. I'd never heard a single word out of her mouth. I thought about the way she'd looked at him and how I felt when she'd said he was beautiful. That simple comment had annoyed me. I think I may have been covetousness. The emotion didn't reside in me, at least I hadn't been aware of it, which is why I couldn't pin it down then. Now, in retrospect, it became clear, but why would I feel covetous about someone who hadn't been mine to begin with, much less in reaction to my married best friend?

"Yeah, it's all coming back to you now, isn't it, Celine?" Her expression mocked me but I just looked at her with apologetic eyes. "Don't look so pitiful. I'm not holding it against you. I'm just happy you're even looking at men again." She chuckled. "I'm going to get started. Get dressed, but after you boink your hot tamale!"

"Get out!" I pushed her towards the door.

She kissed my cheek and exited the bathroom, I

followed. Retrieving her shoes, she slipped out the door. As soon as the lock snapped into place, Santiago's voice filled the room.

"Good morning."

I whipped around.

"Oh! Good morning."

"Sorry, I didn't mean to scare you."

It's a good thing I'd taken the time to brush my teeth while I'd been in the bathroom. He stood and stretched, looking taller to me. He still had on his hat and I wondered how it had stayed in place while he slept.

"Did you tell Kennedy about the break-in?" My face must have revealed my astonishment. "I heard her; she's not very quiet."

Oh, geez. I thought.

"How much did you hear?"

"Enough." His answer had been simple, his smile cunning.

I didn't know what to say to that, but he'd made it easy for me. Trailing a smile behind him, he strolled to the guest bathroom. I ran in the other direction to change clothes, not bothering to shower. We had to get moving. When I returned to the living room, he had a steaming cup of tea waiting for me, while he sipped on coffee, I presumed. His thoughtfulness stunned me. I took a few sips and we headed out the door.

"Sure you don't want a ride?" he gibed.

"Not in this dress."

He laughed as he straddled the motorcycle and put his helmet in place over his hat, fastening the chinstrap. I tossed my bag in the passenger seat. Santiago had replaced all my papers, including those we'd pined over last night, leaving me nothing to pack and nothing to scramble and hide from Kennedy. As I made my way around the rear of his bike towards the driver's seat, Santiago grabbed my wrist. My skin reacted the instant he touched me and so did my heart, picking up pace. I turned around.

"Yeah." The word came out in a squeak. His eyes smiled, but his face remained serious.

"We need to change your locks before we do anything else."

Did he say, "we"?

"I don't have time; I have to meet Kennedy in an hour." His eyes shifted away from me for a quick second.

"Well, I'll do it. I'll take care of it for you and either drop the keys off at your office or meet with you, if that's more convenient."

I had a hard time nailing down my thoughts with chills and heat emanating from the same place. The place where his hand still captured my wrist. I trusted him, beyond reasoning, and he had spent the past two nights with me.

"You don't mind? Wait, don't you have work to do?" I couldn't resist the opportunity to tease him for a change.

"No and yes, but I think my boss lady will make an allowance for this." He winked.

A schoolgirl somewhere inside of me giggled and my insides went to mush. He released his hold on me, well, my arm anyway.

I got in my car and followed him. We didn't spend much time at the library, just long enough for him to confirm what I'd already suspected. The man in the pictures had been Ali and Bryant worked for him. Though his position remained unclear, one thing we knew for sure; it wasn't legitimate.

Outside, I twisted my house key off of the ring and put it into Santiago's palm, careful not to touch him. I didn't want to succumb to the effects he had over me. However, I couldn't control whether or not he touched me. I wore a sleeveless, apricot-colored sundress with an asymmetrical hem and matching pumps. He put his hand on my bare shoulder and dragged it down the length of my arm. I expected tiny fires to spark from each hair follicle as I felt them igniting beneath my skin.

"You're going to be okay, right?" he asked, holding my hand, concern filling the creased lines on his forehead.

"Yeah, I'll be fine."

"Just want to make sure."

"Don't worry. You just get the locks changed. I've got a ton of work to do, an event in a matter of hours, and if I don't leave now, I'll be late meeting Kennedy," I rambled.

"Right. Okay. Well, I'll see you later."

It happened so fast, I didn't have time to see it coming or going. I couldn't even comprehend what had happened despite having been a part of it. We gave each other a swift peck on the lips, turned on our heels and headed to our vehicles. He had dropped my hand moments before, releasing any pretense or inkling of what was about to happen. We kissed in a way that seemed more habitual than romantic, much like the "Honey, I'm home" kiss. Once again, the action oozed comfort and held no awkwardness. Sitting at the wheel, keys dangling in hand, I thought about what had just happened. The sound of his bike roaring by shook me free of the lingering thoughts. As I watched him ride ahead, the dashboard clock came into view. I needed to leave, five minutes ago. A little while later, I stumbled into the coffee house, tousled and windblown.

"That good, huh?" Kennedy poked, before I'd even bent my knees to sit.

"You have no idea!"

She looked stunned for a moment as if she'd

believed me.

"Whatever, Chastity!" She blew off my teasing, sliding a drink over to me. "I bought you an iced mochaccino." I sipped it with a grin.

"I've taken care of the paperwork and already called the vendors. We just need to pick up and set up. Ready?"

"Yes."

We left right away, trying to make the most of our time. I appreciated that she hadn't asked anything more about my morning. I didn't want to talk about Santiago. My emotions were so muddled regarding him and it felt inappropriate to have my emotions involved in the first place, or at all. Kennedy and I were on our way to the gallery to begin setting up for an art gala that would begin before most people had had dinner. My phone rang and Santiago's name popped up on the screen.

"Hi, is everything alright?" I asked, not even giving him the chance to say hello.

"Everything's fine...and you were telling me not to worry. Where are you?"

"On our way to the gallery to set up. Why?"

"Can you give me directions? I'll meet you there so I can give you the new keys."

"Oh, sure." I gave him directions and hung up, a smile dawdling on my lips. Kennedy wore a bigger grin than I did. "Don't say a word!"

She made a motion as though she were zipping her lips and throwing away the key. I knew better; that granted me momentary solace, but she'd pipe up soon enough.

I had expected Santiago to show up soon after we'd arrived at the gallery or maybe I'd just hoped he would. While we were making the final preparations before the guests arrived, I'd found myself stealing glances at the door. The first guests showed up and my anxiety about Santiago's appearance took a back seat. The gallery owner had been pleased with our work as well as the turn out, making his grand re-opening a success. As a new and experimental duty, he'd asked us for help in promoting his event, unchartered territory for us. We decorated, planned, and orchestrated, we didn't advertise. At any rate, from the look of the place and the head count, we could add this to our list of offered services.

"So..." Kennedy began as we browsed some of the artwork on display. "Mr.—"

"He's just dropping off my new keys," I blurted out.

"Your *new* keys? Why are there old ones and why does he have them?"

"Someone broke into the condo, and he suggested I change the locks."

"What!"

"I'll tell you about it later," I said in a low voice, as others browsed alongside us.

They murmured about the extraordinary art, causing me to daydream about what my opening would be like. In my mind, I could see the finished loft. The basement garage converted into show space. Fresh paint still smelled on the walls and the concrete floors lacquered and sealed. A soft jazz played somewhere in the room, just loud enough to notice. Art, my art, lined the walls and sat on easels for admiring eyes and fatted pockets. Soft laughter and hushed conversations waft around the room. The uneasy feeling of being watched snapped me from my fantasy.

Between a two-inch slit among paintings, I caught a man's eye. He looked a familiar. My heart rate excelled in mere seconds. Escalating more from one beat to the next. He didn't care that I'd noticed him staring, but watched me from one gap to the other. He disappeared behind a wall of patrons. I pulled in a breath so sharp it hurt my chest. It took a few more deep breaths to restore the oxygen I'd deprived myself of. For a moment, I wasn't even sure I'd seen the man at all. I felt delusional, as though I were imagining things. I tried to be casual, making my way around the room, searching for him, while having insipid conversations with guests but I didn't see him. Maybe I was losing my mind. At a point, I returned to where Kennedy stood.

"Finally snapped out of it, eh? You were mesmerized by that piece. What's it called? *Catching Clouds*. I don't like it..." She continued to talk, but once again, my ears went deaf to her voice. I swept the room with my eyes, left then right. For a moment, I tuned back in: "Echo, I forgot the other box of draperies in your truck. Do you mind getting them? Mr. Carlson has a special presentation..."

The remainder of her words pelted me in the back as I made a beeline for the door. The fresh air would do me good. Not that anything was "fresh" about California smog. I just needed the vacant space to allow my thoughts to fly away with the wind and, if luck would have me, my sanity would find its way back to me.

Outside and away from the window, I leaned against the building with a thunk and closed my eyes. Unaware of how long I'd stood there, muffled syllables floated to my ears. I opened my eyes, thinking a group of guests were either arriving or departing, but I didn't see anyone. I heard the subdued sound of an urgent conversation. Walking towards my truck, the syllables became more pronounced. The voices sounded angry and terse, but I still had not located where they'd been coming from. So I ignored them and went to retrieve the box as I'd intended to do, feeling as though the smog had made me crazier.

I saw just two drapes in the box, less than what should've been there. Leaning over the back seat, I pulled them out and hung them over my shoulder. When I looked up, I saw two figures through the car window. I recognized Bryant at once. I squinted at the person he argued with and almost fell over the seat. Ali! I couldn't feel my limbs and my breath came out in short, insufficient bursts. Stuck in position, I just froze there, unmoving. Not even my eyes wavered. Ali must have felt me staring at him as I had earlier. His head snapped in my direction and our eyes locked.

My fight or flight instincts clicked just then, and my limbs got the message a lot quicker than my mind. I moved faster than I'd thought I could. I burst into the gallery doors, startling a few of the guests, although not many others seemed to notice. My thoughts reeled. All my senses were heightened but they felt misconstrued. I smelled smoke, saw the reflection of my panic on everyone else's face and I could've sworn I heard Santiago's motorcycle. Wishful thinking, I suppose.

I moved through the crowd, the presence behind me seeming to push me forward. A barrier of people blocked me so I turned to the left, but before I could take another step away from him, he had pulled me aside with feigned gentleness. He mouthed something to me that I didn't understand. Confusion creased my forehead. I realized then, that he had no intention for me to know what he'd said, but made it seem as though he were telling me something that required my attention.

He continued to haul me away, further from eyes and ears. When we were hidden, he slammed his hand over my mouth, shooting panic through my bones and muscles. My eyes stretched wide and body went rigid. I had never thought Bryant held any strength in that scrawny little body, but he'd proved me wrong. My efforts to walk with him had ceased and now he all but dragged me backwards, my limbs like heavy logs.

"Echo," His voice sounded husky as he tried to keep his voice down. "Suffice it to say, we think you know too much. You've proved that."

His bourbon scented words scorched across my cheek. He took a long pause and his hand held hard against my mouth didn't aid my already ragged breathing. He spoke again, but his voice was half an octave softer.

"If you don't give up the goods, they're going to do to my Kennedy, what they did to your Skylar."

A scream caught in my throat and forced its way out through my eyes. I felt the wetness around his fingers and something hard pressed into my side. A gun? I didn't know, I began to feel numb. My blood ran degrees cooler in my veins.

"I love her, Echo. I don't deserve her, but I love her, and I won't lose her because of you!" The edge in his voice had returned.

He stumbled over an obstacle that I could not see and his hand loosened on my mouth. I huffed through his fingers in desperation for more air. My head began to swim. My muscles were losing their rigidity and becoming flaccid. My knees buckled and gave way.

"Hold on, Echo. I've got you," he tried to soothe as he struggled against my unsupported weight.

He lowered me down onto an object and I sat down.

The words he'd just spoken resounded in my ears with familiarity. He'd continued talking, but his last statement played over and again in my head. His words faded into the air as my mind wandered into memories.

I was with Skylar again, as I had been hundreds of times before. We were in his convertible laughing still, when the impact jolted us. I felt him beneath my hand and the wan smile tilting one corner of my mouth. Someone outside of the car spoke to me. Soothing and assuring me. I tried to focus on the fuzzy figure, straining my eyes. My vision sharpened at the exact moment he spoke again. *How did he know my name?* I thought. Bryant's words sounded again and again, and his face came clear into view. I saw him hovering over me amidst the shattered glass, his eyes shifting between Skylar and me. His expression frightened me and the corner of my mouth drooped downward. How had he gotten here so fast? Kennedy had said he'd been at the country club waiting for us. So how was he here? I snapped into awareness, back into the present and his words came into cognizance.

"He wasn't supposed to die! The accident was just supposed to scare him. They said if I didn't do it, it would be Kennedy. I was in a lot deeper than I wanted to be, but by then I had no choice. It was supposed to be simple and easy. No one was supposed to get hurt." He rambled. Aghast, I teetered on the brink of fainting.

"Skylar was supposed to invest a few bucks, everyone get their share and that's it. I don't know what went wrong. How things got so messy and the money...

Dammit, Skylar!" he yelled. I went rigid with fear again. He wasn't stable and neither was I. "I didn't mean to kill him! He was my best friend. He wasn't supposed to die!" Tears fell from his eyes but they evaporated in almost the same moment they'd appeared. "They can't have Kennedy! So you'd better—"

"Echo?"

Kennedy's voice cut off Bryant as she burst into the small storage area where he'd dragged me. He had set me on a crate but I huffed still, my breathing erratic, as though I'd never stopped running.

"What's going on here? I've been looking for you. Someone told me you were in a consult and I came to check on you. Bryant, why are you back here? You shouldn't be here. Carlson would have a fit if he found out. Echo, what's the matter?"

Her last question came out in a slow drawl. Confusion and concern twisted her face and her eyes darted in several directions, trying to make sense of the scene, I presumed. Bryant had snatched his hand from my lips the moment the door parted from its seal.

"I was trying to calm her down," Bryant lied, placing his hand on my back.

I flinched away from his touch with such revolt that I almost fell off the crate. All of a sudden, Santiago stood between Bryant and me. I hadn't even noticed him in the room, but his scent brought his presence into focus.

I *had* heard his motorcycle. His eyes burned with rage, and his body tensed. Kennedy stood stalk still, seeming not to know what to do. However, it just took one moment.

"Santiago," she spoke to him but kept her eyes trained on Bryant. "Get her out of here...now! I've got my assistant; I can close this event." At last, she looked at Santiago. "Use the back door. I don't want anyone seeing her like this. As for the drunken buzzard here, I'll call him a cab."

I opened my mouth to say something, but hadn't enough air to breathe, let alone speak.

"We'll talk later, okay?" Kennedy said in a soft voice as she gazed at me. Then she shot an angry look at Bryant. As we walked by, she brushed back my hair with her fingers. "I love you."

I nodded and Santiago ushered me out without one word or probing question, a trait I had very well fallen in love with. I heard Kennedy and Bryant arguing, until the door shut behind us. Santiago had parked his bike on the sidewalk just beyond the gallery window, which couldn't be legal. He helped me onto the rear seat of the motorcycle and placed the helmet atop my head. He fastened the chin strap in place and put a pair of clear glasses over my puffy eyes. He straddled the machine in front of me and took my hands, wrapping my arms around his midsection. I felt like a marionette doll, freezing in whatever position he'd placed me in. The engine roared to life sending a jolt through me, but I didn't feel afraid. All the fear had been left in the gallery storage room. I gave no thought to anything. I just sat there.

"Hold on." Santiago didn't utter any other words for a while.

We cruised little known streets for a time before entering the freeway. Then he increased speed, pulling my arms a little tighter around him. His instincts were impeccable. He had known not to take me home, the last place I wanted to be. As we rode the freeway at a speed I'd rather not know, a feeling of exhilaration began to wash over me. Surroundings flashed by in blurs of streaking color. Night had fallen and, where there was light, it illuminated those blurs. The comfort Santiago always brought with him settled in and I laid my head against his back.

The crowded, colliding thoughts I'd had were zipping away, ten at a time with each indistinct form that whizzed by. The wind licked my face and whisked my hair into a tangle of flying curls behind us. The cool breeze ran circles around my bare legs while the hem of my dress played peek-a-boo with my thighs. I took a smooth, deep breath in and exhaled with ease. Then, I did it again. Moving at this pace through time had an effect on me.

For about two years, I had been stuck in a stagnant sea of the unknown, fighting a rip current of pending misery and drowning in waves of sporadic sorrow. On occasion, I felt that I'd rather drown than continue a fight I may never win. This moment, however, felt very different.

For the first time since losing Skylar, I could breathe; as if I were, at long last, coming up for air. The moment hadn't been the most befitting considering what I'd just learned. My best friend's spouse murdered my husband and now he'd threatened not only my life, but hers as well. I closed my eyes and inhaled again, releasing a slow exhale. Breathing. How often we take it for granted.

Nine

I couldn't guess at how long we'd been riding, but I noticed we'd slowed down quite a bit. At first, I'd been less than aware of Santiago's presence, until all at once I felt the sensation of his ribs against the insides of my arms; his taut abs under my wrists and hands; and one of his large hands resting on my left leg. His fingers caressed my skin and I wondered how long his hand had been there, for his warmth had settled into my muscles.

We exited the 101 and pulled up to a red light. He'd removed his hand, but the heat remained. I lifted my head from its resting place and looked around. I wasn't familiar with my surroundings at all. I had no idea where we were. Santiago must have sensed my insecurity because he reached back and gave my thigh a reassuring pat. I looked to my right and saw a sign that read Salinas. We were in Salinas, California. I'd been in such a blithe state of mind I hadn't noticed where we were headed.

It hadn't felt as if we'd been riding long enough to get to Salinas, a small city about two hours outside of San Francisco. We stopped at a gas station and grabbed some snacks and a couple of drinks. Santiago got on first and then extended his hand to aid me. I took his hand, threw my leg over the seat and grasped the opposite hand waiting on the other side, giving me leverage to sit down gently. I sandwiched our bag of goodies between us, and we were off again.

I didn't know where we were going, but Santiago did. He appeared to be familiar with the area. A few blocks away, we stopped again at a small open area. It didn't look much like a park, but I suppose that's what it was. Benches lined the outer perimeter of the grassy circle in front of a paved walk. Dated street lamps measured a distance one to another. Aged oak trees provided glorious shade on a hot summer's day, I'm sure, but tonight they provided the cover of shadows.

We seated ourselves on a bench and I folded my bare feet under me, leaving my shoes perched on the seat of the bike. Neither of us spoke right away, guzzling our drinks instead. We exchanged snacks and looked around at the scenery.

"Hola, Morenita," Santiago broke the silence.

He ran the pad of his soft thumb along the line of my jaw and pinched my chin. I knew what hola meant, but the other word had been lost upon me. From his inflection, I figured it to be a term of endearment. My face felt hot, blushing from his words and his touch. Something about his tone and the tender adoration veiling his face brought my shyness to the surface.

"Hi, Santiago."

I'd experienced such a sense of tranquility around him but also, I'd often feel things at polar-opposite ends of the spectrum. Extreme annoyance or intense serenity. His spirit often set me off or set me at ease. There didn't seem to be a middle ground—no gray area. Whatever I felt, magnified every time I saw him, every time I spent time with him. I enjoyed our comfortable silences, our nonverbal exchanges, and the way he read my thoughts.

"I got lost here once," he said. "I needed a release and I just hopped on my bike and hit the 101, not even paying attention to the direction I'd been going. The day before had been difficult. It was Helena's birthday, April eighteenth. She'd turned two and I'd called Cristina, hoping to wish her a happy birthday. She'd already returned the gifts I'd sent, just to upset me. We argued about nothing. At least nothing that mattered." His eyes were dim, sad. "You know, I don't even know what she looks like. She won't send pictures...nothing."

I took hold of his hand. He ran his index finger across the tiny veins at my wrist. My eyes settled where our skin met. Despite the summer sun, his skin looked pale, compared to the shade the sun had granted me, even visible under the localized light of the lamp.

"People think motorcycles are so dangerous, but that thing has saved my life—and the lives of others— many days. Whatever I'm feeling, I can ride until I'm numb." He had a far off look in his eyes, as though he were dreaming.

Listening to him speak of riding and having just experienced the numbness, I understood. I'd never fathomed in any way, dream or fantasy, that I'd one day find myself on the back of a motorcycle, let alone enjoy it.

"Anyway, this is where I ended up that day. I just rode without thinking, without a destination."

"Painting used to do that for me. I haven't picked up a brush in ages. When I paint, I forget the world. All that exists is me, the paint, and the canvas." I took my turn gazing into nothingness.

"You're smiling," he observed.

I snapped out of my trance and popped another piece of candy into my mouth. We were still holding hands.

"So you ended up here and came back on purpose?" I looked around at the little square. He chuckled.

"Yeah and I've dragged you with me."

"So you have," I said around a laugh.

We continued to talk without inhibitions. We discussed most everything. Everything except for the event that had brought us to this harmonious setting. Somewhere in the middle of all the words that floated around us, I'd unfolded and stretched my legs out in front of me. My ankles crisscrossed each other as they rested on Santiago's thighs. His hands found a place on my shin as we continued to talk and he'd stroke my calf in increments. Our conversation seemed endless. In time, light streaked the skyline with bright color and we still hadn't run out of things to say. The little shops all around us became visible. Dots of lighted windows appeared, evidence of the morning risers.

"Come on." Santiago gave my leg a light slap.

I stretched long before walking the few feet back to the bike. We took a short ride to a bed and breakfast, both of which sounded like heaven to me. I couldn't figure which I wanted more, the bed or the breakfast. He paid for a single room in the Victorian styled retreat and spa. The place had gaudy decor, but beautiful in its own right. The room boasted dramatic draperies, heavy and well made, hand-carved furniture etched in gold, and a flat screen television. It was a visible oxymoron. I climbed right into bed among the plush linens and cloud-like pillows. A long sigh escaped me and that's the last thing I remembered. Somewhere mid-sigh I thought I'd heard Santiago say something about breakfast, tainting my dreams with dancing eggs and sausages.

I awoke in his arms. This wasn't the first time, and

it seemed as though it wouldn't be the last. I couldn't figure out the time of day by the fading sunlight. The arm wedged between us also held my watch. I tried to wriggle it free but did not succeed.

"It's a quarter to seven," Santiago whispered. *How did he do that!*

"In the morning?"

"No, mi amor. In the evening."

"Oh my gosh! What?" I snapped up. We had slept the day away.

"Don't panic."

Too late. I thought.

"I called Kennedy this morning, and she got her assistant to fill in for you. Since you left your phone, purse, and briefcase, she has everything she needs to get the job done. I told her we'll be back tomorrow in time for the party."

"Thank you," I couldn't think of anything else to say. At a loss for any other words, I relaxed back into his arms.

It had not dawned on me that I'd left with nothing. Had I even closed the trunk to my car? Doubtful. Thank God for both Kennedy and Santiago. I shook off the thoughts of the previous night, not willing to deal with them just yet.

"It's no problem. I figured that would be the first thing you'd concern yourself with, and I didn't want to wake you."

"What about you? I'm sure you have better things to do than to babysit me."

"Other things, yes. Better things, no. I'm right where I want to be and right where I'm needed."

I couldn't object to that. My eyes took in the room again, as if for the first time. As with all the furnishings, the large dresser was quite ostentatious. Upon it sat a breakfast tray with a half-eaten meal, cold by now, for sure. Breakfast in bed again, how fortunate for me. This time, however, I had slept right through it. I shifted from his arms.

"Where are you going?" he asked, reaching for me.

"I need a shower."

"I bought some clothes for you, nothing fancy. Not much to choose from around here. Just some jeans and a t-shirt and a pair of sandals. I didn't buy any underwear. I wasn't sure what you'd like and I would have chosen something inappropriate. So," a sly grin spread across his face. "I guess you'll have to go commando."

I imagined the visuals running through his mind and picked up a throw pillow from a chair and hurled it at him. He caught it as if we were playing a game of catch. I shook my head and snatched the new clothes from the back of the chair where he'd hung them, stomping into the bathroom with mock offense. I couldn't hide or hinder the smile that formed as I stepped into the shower.

The water beaded my back and made streams down my legs. Steam clouded the glass enclosure, but my thoughts ran clear. The realization of how I'd come to this moment pelted me like every drop of water. The all too real reasons why I'd ended up in this tiny town. The confession that had changed the accidental death of my husband to a homicide. I lifted my face to the spray and submerged myself. The water camouflaged my tears well, even from me. The transformation from quiet tears to violent sobs shocked me. My body rocked with the ferocity of weeping I could not control. I crumpled in a heap on the shower floor, curling into myself. Santiago knocked at the door.

"Echo," he called out to me. I couldn't answer. *Bam! Bam! Bam!* "Echo!" His voice sounded urgent but he paused for a moment. I hoped he would go away, leave me to cry myself into a coma, right here.

"I'm coming in," he announced.

I didn't object. I didn't move. I didn't speak. The tears choked me, cutting off my airway, and my words, that is, if I were able to form any. Seconds felt like minutes, but Santiago stayed with me. He had seated himself next to me on the tile under the cascading water and enveloped me with his arms. I felt his clothes, rough on my bare, heated skin, first dry and then wet. He just let me cry and I did. We stayed there; I in his lap, he cradling me like a fragile creature until the water ran cold. I didn't notice that he had covered me with a towel. I assumed that fabric to be a part of his clothing. He carried me out of the shower and replaced the wet towel with a dry robe before sitting me down on the lounge chair in the room.

"Bryant killed my Skylar." I choked the words out of my mouth.

"What did you say?" In the middle of towel drying my hair, he stopped.

"He told me, at the gala, that he'd caused the accident." I couldn't bring myself to use the word kill again. It sounded so vile in the same sentence with Skylar.

"Is that what happened back there?"

"Yes, I saw him outside talking to Ali."

"Ali was there?" He raised his voice.

"Yes, I thought Ali had followed me inside, but it was Bryant."

I recounted the events of the night to him as well as I could recall. His anger boiled, but my hurt overruled any anger I may have had. I didn't have enough space to harbor both at the same time.

Crying had left me drained. Even if I had wanted to eat, I don't think I could've found the strength to chew. I crawled back into bed, into Santiago's arms. His fingers danced in my hair while he hummed another soft song. Before surrendering again to slumber, we'd agreed to take this matter to the police. The time had come.

"But first, there's something else we must do tomorrow," Santiago said.

The request came out of nowhere, although, I suspected it hadn't been a request at all. Maybe he'd been speaking to me already and that had been all I'd heard. What could be more important than what we had just discussed?

We awoke with the sun. My stomach, at once, protested against the emptiness. Thank goodness the place had an early bird breakfast. I exchanged the soft robe for the jeans and t-shirt Santiago had bought for me. Each garment fit as though tailored for my body. I wondered how he'd chosen the correct sizes. Dress sizes were different from pant sizes but he'd been spot on in his selection. I'd even liked the cute shirt, but I wished he had bought some underwear, inappropriate or not. Since he hadn't, I had no choice but to go "commando" and it felt liberating, almost sexy, in a sneaky, I-have-a-secret kind of way.

We went to the dining area to eat. Santiago had brought our helmets along so we departed right after our meal and went for a cruise around town. Relief blew over me like the wind. I wasn't sure if I'd felt relieved because I knew we'd go to the police or if the motorcycle had just been doing its magic. It could've been both. I knew Bryant would be exposed and some kind of justice would begin. Skylar deserved it and, to be frank, so did I.

My thoughts had come and gone with such speed, I'd almost forgotten I'd had any thoughts at all. Santiago rubbed my leg again and slowed the bike down. He'd driven us to Old Town Salinas, which I considered funny, for it all seemed like an old town to me. Santiago gave my thigh two taps, signaling for me to dismount. He helped me off and backed the bike into a gap that didn't appear wide enough for us to stand in let alone squeeze a bike into. I watched him park and while he did, I got a look at the label on the bike. Screamin' Eagle, it read, by Harley Davidson, an apt name to describe such a loud machine. The bike was green and sparkling and chrome all over. The handlebars looked as if they belonged on a jungle gym rather than a motorcycle. I'd never seen one quite like it, but then again, they'd all looked the same to me before now.

"Psst."

I looked up at Santiago, having been in a daze, standing there with my helmet on.

"You gonna take that thing off or what? I admit you look cute, but it's not really necessary for walking." By now he'd released the chin fastener and removed it for me. "You're not that clumsy, are you?"

"Depends on what day it is."

We were at an outdoor farmer's market. The array of edible colors filled the air with a tantalizing aroma. Santiago took hold of my hand and pulled me forward, interlacing our fingers. We strolled the market while he whispered into my ears, making me laugh in the faces of vendors. As we browsed, we'd engaged in lighthearted conversation, shared bites of fresh, delicious produce, and laughed until we were both red.

"I've got a bit of a surprise for you," he said.

"Okay..." I elongated the word, my skepticism apparent.

"Don't be such a scaredy cat. You don't think I'd let anything happen to you, do you?"

I don't know why but, I didn't.

"Yeah, well..." I teased. He looked at me with feigned irritation.

"Vamos mujer!"

He led us back to the bike. 'Let's go, woman' I translated in my head, laughing as I skipped along, trying to keep pace with him. We inched out of the tight space and rode for a short while until we arrived somewhere I'd never expected to be.

"Surprise!" He turned back to say to me.

"What!"

"I said, 'surprise!'"

"You're kidding me, right? No way! We're going to the rodeo?"

"Yep! I thought it would be nice to have a little fun before we head back. It's clear, you've never been."

He'd been so full of surprises. I didn't know anyone who'd been to a rodeo, much less attended one myself. I couldn't think of anything else to say, but Santiago oozed enthusiasm.

The makeshift parking lot was all dust and gravel, clouding the air with it as we rolled to a stop. He leaned the bike onto the kickstand and we got off.

"Hop on," Santiago suggested.

I laughed, ignoring him as he stood in front of me with his back turned so that I'd hop on his back, a tempting offer. I had on a pair of barely-there flip-flops, but he couldn't have been serious.

"Come on. I don't want you to hurt your feet. It would be just like you to get a rock stuck under your toe, sever it and then we'd have to spend the rest of the day in the emergency room."

"Shut up!" That's the best comeback I could come up with, but he hadn't been far off.

At the end of a sigh, I climbed onto his back, feeling like a nine-year-old girl. He held my shoes in his hands and walked to the gate, as if he didn't have the extra pounds on his back.

"What are you, my bucking bronco?" I joked.

"If you want me to be." His suggestive tone had not been lost upon me.

I slapped his chest but couldn't help but laugh. I'd set myself up for that one.

"You asked!" He laughed, setting me down on the pavement after putting my shoes in place first.

Once we'd found seats my excitement peaked, having risen like the roar of the crowd between the parking lot and walking around. I had no idea what to expect, providing a bit of a thrill. We both sat in anticipation and watched the first event. I shrieked for the cowboys who'd thrown themselves in front of the bucking horses and the ones who'd fell off of them.

I'd enjoyed the rodeo so much, it surprised me. It's nothing I would have chosen for myself but I'd had the best time. I couldn't decide if I'd liked one thing about it more than the other, perhaps, except one. However, I wasn't willing to admit it—even within my private thoughts.

Santiago gave me another bronco ride through the parking lot and sat me down on the seat of the bike. From there we went back to the room to check out. He had even bought a little backpack for us to put our things in. He had thought of everything and that impressed me...more. The ride back to our civilization brought a more euphoric mood than the last. I found a pocket of coziness to snuggle into and dwelled there. Santiago's hand became a permanent fixture on my thigh. Still, an endowed sense of wonder accompanied me and this entire scene. To anyone else, this probably didn't look strange at all. Maybe even ordinary. For me, however, it had been something to marvel at and such an out-of-character experience.

We stopped at a gas station, just outside of San Francisco, and I bounced as I walked into the store. While I mulled over what type of drink to get, Santiago walked up behind me.

"Hola, Morenita." I turned to him, my smile unhindered.

"What does that mean?"

"Morenita?" he asked.

I nodded.

"It means: my brown-skinned girl." He slid a tendril of my hair between his fingers.

"Hmm." A spark burst inside of me.

"What? Does that bother you?"

"No. I—I think I like it." I crinkled my nose on one side.

Returning my eyes to his, I observed his steady gaze. He'd wrapped one arm around my waist and his fingers toyed with the ends of my pigtail at the nape of my neck.

"What?" I asked.

I felt the goofy grin on my face but he didn't answer me, he just stared. Adapting his way, I didn't press him for an answer. I just waited. He squinted a bit before he spoke, tilting his head to the side.

"I never noticed the flecks of green in your eyes," he paused, his eyes unwavering. "I mean, I know they're hazel, but the green is a new to me. I've never seen it before now."

A single tear tried to fight its way to the surface as I watched him scrutinize my eyes. He may not have been able to define it, but of course, I knew what the green in my eyes meant.

"My eyes turn green when I'm happy," I whispered, more to myself than to him.

Santiago broadened his smile, hugged me, and planted a kiss on my neck. It tickled, making me giggle. My laughter caused his smile to spread. When he pulled away, in that moment, his beauty became apparent to me. I looked at him, as if for the first time. The way the corners of his face crinkled when he smiled. How his long, curled lashes, framed his ever twinkling eyes. The tiny mole which dotted the right side of his bottom lip. His creamy, smooth skin beneath his minimal facial hair. He looked so much younger than his years, enhanced by the wavy ponytail he wore at the back of his neck.

My attraction to him grew, all of a sudden, astounding me. It seemed to come out of nowhere. He stood so close, I could smell him with every intake of breath, intensifying what I'd felt. *God, he's sexy!* I felt my ears grow hot and I pictured them blazing red at the tops. The heat spread, fast. I turned from him and opened the cooler door. God knows I needed the cold air. I'd closed my eyes while I stood in the cooler but fluttered them open after a few seconds, trying to concentrate long enough to choose a drink.

Santiago stood close to me, too close. My heart raced so fast and hard, it caused physical pain. I couldn't take it anymore. I snatched the first beverage within arm's reach and spun around in the opened door.

I wondered if my ears were still red or if the color had, instead, flooded my face. My skin had chilled, but my insides hoarded fire. I parted my lips to speak, but I never had a chance. Provided any words were able to form in the first place, they wouldn't have made it out. I never saw him move, but I felt him with a palpability I couldn't mistake for illusion.

He'd let my ponytail loose from its confines, my hair draping around my shoulders. The heat had returned to my left ear, thanks to Santiago's hand covering it. His long fingers twisted in my hair, massaging my scalp and my lips seared from the heat of his mouth upon mine. He had drawn our bodies into a tight press, but I had stumbled backwards into the cooler. I felt the cold objects on my back but Santiago generated a temperature that didn't allow me to be cold, or even cool. My left hand ascended, on its own accord, gliding from his forearm to his shoulder, ending in a stroke at the back of his neck. He pushed me farther into the oversized refrigerator with a tender increase in pressure at the lips. The drink I held slipped from my fingers but I never heard the sound it made. I assumed it hit the floor, it hadn't anywhere else to go. Feeling unsteady, I tried to brace myself by pushing against the icy, cold glass door with my free hand, streaking the condensation we'd produced.

The moment went on forever, it seemed, yet not long enough. He pulled away from me with tangible reluctance. In spite of the cold, Santiago had beaded sweat at his temples. We both seemed a little dazed as we looked around, noticing that we'd fogged most of the cooler doors. We laughed and I used the distraction to move away from him, before we steamed up the remainder of the glass. Santiago picked up the fallen drink and replaced it, retrieving two more from a colder area.

When we got to the cashier, she looked more besotted than I'd felt. She had obviously seen the torrid display. Feeling self-conscious, I put my fingers over my tender lips. Though she didn't speak, her expression said plenty. Santiago paid for our drinks and gas. I just stood there trying to avoid her eyes. She'd been so busy gawking at us that she gave Santiago a sharpie marker to sign the receipt with, instead of a pen. He made no qualms about it and signed his name but, prior to returning the marker to old starry eyes, he took my hand, palm up. He turned his back to me, shifted his body in front of mine and clamped my arm beneath his. A soft tickle traced my palm. *What could he possibly be writing that he couldn't say to me?* I already have his phone number. It felt like just a few letters, so it couldn't say much. He blew the ink dry, folded my hand closed, and held my fist in his hand.

"No peeking," he told me.

As curious as I'd been, I obeyed anyway. He kept my fist tucked close to him so I couldn't look. Once we got going again, forgetting about his secret message had been easy. We arrived in San Francisco, later than we'd anticipated, so Santiago brought me to Kennedy's office, instead of the police station. Besides that, I still needed my briefcase which had all the 'evidence' we'd needed to show them. We hopped off his motorcycle and I removed the helmet, placing it on the seat.

"Do you need me to pick you up later?" he asked.

"Could you? I'll need to go home, shower, and change. Kennedy and Sherri can hold down the fort long enough for me to do that. We'll get all the leg work done now."

"No problem." He smiled.

"You're the best!" I smiled too.

His fingers ran a path from my elbow to my wrist until my hand rested inside his. He took his other hand and, with the softest touch, smoothed my palm open, stretching out each of my fingers. I looked down at our hands and at the revealed scribe he'd marked there. I knew he hadn't written much, that is, until I read the two words and comprehended their meaning. 'Te Amo' it read. I stared at the heavy black ink in my hand for a long time and a tear fell into my palm. I looked up, searching his eyes for confirmation, not that I needed any. He dried my cheek where the tear had streaked a path of its own. I pressed my forehead to the center of his chest and put my hands on either side of his waist. I could not respond. I didn't know what to say. I didn't know what to feel or how I'd felt. He cupped my head in his hands and kissed the top of my head.

"Alright, get to work!" He nudged me in the direction of the building. "Go on. I'll see you in a little bit, okay. Get some work done."

How could I work holding the weight of these words in my hand?

"Okay," I agreed. "7:30."

"See you then."

He gave me a peck on the lips and readied himself to leave. I walked inside, in a fog of rapture. He watched after me, and when the door shut me in, he sped away.

Ten

I floated into Kennedy's office building, a goofy smile pasted on my face.

"Hi, Echo," said Sherri.

"Hi, Sherri." I'd called her name in one day more than I had all year. I popped my head into Kennedy's office. "Ms. Keigle."

"Echo," she waved me inside. "Close the door."

A strange energy hovered around her. Standing behind her desk, she hadn't smiled when I walked in and her eyes were cold, uninviting. I almost backed out of the room, but I didn't. After shutting the door behind me with a light click, I turned around.

"What the hell is this?" she asked in a clipped

voice.

She had slammed a pile of papers on her desk and they'd fanned out, making most of them visible. She'd wasted no time getting to the point. I looked at her desk, filled with pictures and then back at her. She stewed in a few emotions, all evident from her expression and reddened eyes. I had dreaded this moment from the time I'd discovered Skylar's hidden box; the day I'd have to tell my best friend of twenty years, that her husband is not who she'd thought. Tears sprang to my eyes the instant I inhaled to speak. I exhaled a shaky breath and pressed the intercom button on her desk phone. Kennedy never moved, her eyes just followed me and a tear fell from her eye.

"Sherri, hold all Kennedy's calls and no interruptions until further notice." I said into the speaker.

"Sure thing."

I wanted Kennedy to sit down, but I knew better than to ask her to. I didn't know where to begin, so I decided to explain the pictures first.

"A private investigator took those pictures. Skylar had hired him." My voice came out hushed, sullen. "The guy with Bryant is named Jahi Ali. Ali has been running investment scams and Bryant had talked Skylar into getting involved without revealing the illegal part of it. That's where all the money came from and then things started to go awry. Skylar started researching but he'd never had the chance to get any answers. Now, they want the money back and Bryant is trying to get it."

I continued talking for what felt like hours.

My emotions drained with every word. Fact after shocking fact, Kennedy got closer to her chair, until she plopped down into it. She sat there, blinking her eyes time and again as my explanations continued. I'd expected her to interject or argue, but she didn't, making me wonder if she believed me. I'd had a hard time believing it all myself. I'd told her about the notes, the death of the investigator, the phony company, Ali's appearance at the gala, and about Bryant's drunken confession.

When I'd finished, we both cried, after which we sat in silence. Her eyes, dull and void of the vibrancy I'd become accustomed to seeing, she, at last, said something.

"Well, that explains a lot." She paused, taking a long, unstable breath. "That explains...everything. Bryant has been acting so strange the past few months. With the anniversary of Skylar's death being so near, I thought maybe that could be it but I could not have been more wrong. He's been protective, too protective. It's not his way. He's so passive, a lot of the time I'm left wondering if anything concerns him at all. He even took my keys the other day. I don't know if he was trying to make sure I didn't go anywhere or what."

"Wait, Bryant had your keys? When?"

"The day before the gallery opening. He must have forgotten that I'd hidden spares around the house. He made a big stink about it."

"Oh my gosh!" My hand flew to my mouth.

"What?" Kennedy's eyes grew wide.

"That's the same day someone broke into my house. I never got the chance to tell you about it. Santiago had come to my place that evening and that's why he was on the couch when you showed up the next morning. The cops said whomever broke in may have used a key." I paused. "No one has a key except you."

"You think Bryant did it?"

"Considering everything else...yes. He was looking for the money. I'm sure of it."

I could see the denial beginning to creep up on her. I couldn't blame her. I'd never before seen Bryant as a thief nor dangerous, but all that had changed.

"Kennedy. I'm sorry about all this and I know it's hard to believe, but I'm not making this up. That's why I didn't tell you sooner. I wanted to make sure I had more facts. I would never have thought Bryant capable of any of this...of hurting Sky. If he hadn't told me himself, I wouldn't believe it." I took a deep breath and sighed. "He was there, Kennedy. Bryant had been the first person at the scene of the accident. He talked to me, tried to keep me alert, even before the cops showed up."

"Why didn't you tell me that? I mean, back then? I thought it was insane how fast he'd gotten there when we were at the same place. He'd told me he was in the men's locker room. I just figured he reacted faster than I did. Things went south in a hurry, so I never thought about it much beyond that."

That solidified it for me. Bryant had never gone to the country club.

"I didn't know it'd been him at first. I'd lost a lot of blood and everything looked hazy, but I remember his voice and what he'd said. He said the same words to me at the gallery. His face became clear for a second before I passed out."

"This is all too much." Kennedy fiddled with something on her desk.

"I know. Believe me, I've been trying to come to grips with it myself but you should know, we are going to the cops..."

"What?" Her head snapped up in surprise. "And who the hell is 'we'!"

"I've been sitting on this too long already and Bryant is in over his head. If Ali can persuade Bryant to do things we would have never thought possible, there is no telling what else he's capable of. I'm surprised Ali didn't come after me at the gallery."

She huffed, looking overwhelmed. I'd had time to take it all in; she'd been forced to take it all in one gulp. Her shoulders slumped forward and I knew what that meant.

She couldn't deny it. She knew, as well as I did, going to the authorities was the right thing to do. I pulled my chair around to her side of the desk and put my arms around her shoulders.

"I'm so sorry, honey," I crooned.

"You know Bryant and I argued at the gallery before I poured him into a cab. He told me the accident had been his fault. I blew it off, thinking his drunken guilt had gotten the best of him. I still don't want to believe it and I don't know if I do, but listening to you and putting it all together..." she trailed off. "The next day he acted as if nothing had happened. Then I found all this in your attaché case and didn't know what to think. I knew, on some level, that he'd done something that wasn't quite right, but I just chalked it up to bad deals or company problems, but nothing like this. I should be the one apologizing to you."

"It's not your fault. I know you had no idea and neither did I. He'd fooled all of us, including Skylar. I'm still having trouble believing it, but the fingers are pointing in his direction, even his own. What I can say is, he's trying to keep you safe."

"By sacrificing someone else? How noble!" she screamed. We'd gotten past the denial stage and had forded into anger.

"Well, soon this will all be out in the open and in the hands of the authorities. I just hope they find Ali too, so no one else has to go through this. They should throw away the key this time."

We had a few more minutes of silence, wiping our faces and refreshing our makeup. We'd gone from shedding tears to tossing around jokes. It seemed strange behavior given the circumstances, but it had always helped us cope when things got tough. Besides, everyone preferred laughter over tears.

We also had an event to host and couldn't walk around a party with swollen, teary eyes. Before long, we'd dropped the weight of the situation and picked up a lighter load. We had a party to plan.

"What the hell is that on your hand?" Kennedy interrupted my re-enactment of a joke I'd been telling her since we were kids. "No pen and paper in farm country?"

I looked at my hand to see what she'd meant. I had forgotten about the inscription and she didn't even give me a chance to open my mouth. She jerked my hand towards her face to read it.

"Te Amo." She looked to me. "Doesn't that mean I love you?" She didn't wait for me to answer. "Oh my God! Echo! Motorcycle Muchacho is in love with you!"

Hearing the proclamation out loud suspended all my thoughts. An image of Santiago replaced everything else, his tantalizing eyes drinking me in.

"Well, what did you say? Did you say it back? That must've been a hell trip to corn country. Did you two sleep together, I mean for real this time? Wait, *do you love him?*"

I chose to answer the least rhetorical question.

"I don't know if I love him or not. I do like him. He's so thoughtful and takes care of me in a way that I haven't experienced in a long time."

I couldn't hear myself anymore, but the vibration in my chest signaled that I'd continued talking. My eyes lost focus while parts of me infused with glee and my mouth ambled ahead of my mind.

"Holy hiccups, you *do* love him!" Kennedy all but yelled, interrupting my babble.

"What? No! I said I don't know."

"I heard what your mouth said, but your everything else says love."

She stretched out the word love the same way she did when we were eleven and I liked some boy...any boy.

"Whatever." I waved her off and reached over to press the intercom button on her desk phone again. "Sherri, we are reopened for business."

"Great. I've gotten everything taken care of. Whenever you two are ready, we can get going," Sherri said in her squeaky, little voice.

"Thanks, Sher, you're the best. Three minutes," Kennedy answered, shutting off the intercom, turning to me. "You have to tell me all about your little excursion."

"Will do, but not now. Let's move. I still have to go home and shower. I don't want to offend anyone."

We laughed together. It felt good now that I wasn't withholding such a heavy secret from her. I gathered up all the papers from her desk and returned them to my case and we were set to leave. Walking through the door, Kennedy turned to me.

"Do you need me to take you home to change?" she offered. "Sorry, I parked the truck at your house, instead of here."

"No, it's okay. We don't have time now. Besides, I told Santiago to pick me up at seven-thirty. Since he changed the locks, he's the only one with keys. He came to the gallery to drop them off, but I never got them. We couldn't get in if we wanted to." She gave me an accusatory look. "Shut up!"

"First of all, we *could* get in! And 'B,' if you would just admit you love him, maybe I will shut up. He has keys to your place! I damned near had to steal mine. In fact, I think I did."

"It's not as if he's moving in, Kennedy. Geez!"

"Close enough!"

I sighed with a smile. We were on our way and in hyper drive since we'd spent so much time at the office. We'd gotten everything done in record time, thanks to Sherri's preparations.

Seven thirty came fast and I heard Santiago's approach—me and everyone else. That bike owned up to its name. I watched from the window as he pulled up to the curb like a law-abiding citizen. I held up one finger to him and mouthed "One minute." He gave me a simple nod and turned off the engine and I scrambled to complete a couple of tasks before finding Kennedy.

"I'll be back in an hour, maybe less. I'll try to make it less." The words tumbled out, but she netted every one of them. After all, she spoke much faster than I did.

"Okay, hun."

"Be back in a flash. Love you!" I turned on my heel to leave.

"Hey, Echo?" Kennedy called.

"Yeah?" I turned to face her.

"Don't trip and fall on anything, okay."

"I'll be fine." I noticed her mischievous expression and caught her meaning. She had not been speaking of my clumsy nature at all. "You are deplorable!"

She laughed as I strode away, shaking my head. I bounded out the door to Santiago. Although I'd seen him just hours ago, I'd missed him. He smiled when I walked out the door, an adequate "hello," if you asked me. I hopped on the back of the bike as if it were the most normal, everyday thing for me. I supposed that's what it'd become.

"Beautiful," he said.

"Mmm," I sighed, kissing his neck.

I donned my helmet and glasses and wrapped my arms around his waist, pulling myself close to him and giving him a squeeze. He caressed my arms before starting the engine. We merged into traffic and headed towards my place. At a stop light, he turned his head to the side.

"What festivities are we hosting this evening?" he asked.

"A swanky bachelorette party."

"That should be fun. Strippers?" He chuckled.

"None that I've ordered." I chuckled with him.

When we pulled into my garage, Santiago parked beside my truck, rather than behind it as he'd done before. We scurried to get upstairs, an effort for me since we never rushed when we were together, leaving time to worry about itself. He led the way since he had the keys. When we got to my front door, Santiago pulled up short. He'd had the key firm in hand, aimed at the lock but he didn't put it in the slot. Afraid to say anything, to move, to blink, I stood there waiting for a cue from him. He leaned a little to the side and then turned around, not making a sound. It felt like déjà vu but, unlike before, I heard audible noises coming from my unit. Whoever had broken into my unit was still in there.

"*Shh,*" he signed.

He put his lips to my ear, making me warm in some places. The heat spread to my cheeks, quite inappropriate considering the severity of the situation.

"Go to the lobby," he whispered, his breath tickling the fine hairs on my skin. I couldn't help but scrunch my shoulder up to my ear. "Alert security. Call the police. Run!"

The last word struck a chord of trepidation. I searched his stern eyes and he pointed, jabbing his finger in the direction I should've already been running. His body had shifted just enough for me to see what had stopped him from unlocking the door. Gaping holes stood where the locks had been. Splintered wood littered the floor, fanned in various directions. Santiago gave me an impatient look and I took off down the hall.

The elevator couldn't come fast enough. As I headed for the stairs the elevator bell dinged. I pivoted on my heels, running in the other direction and slipped through the doors before they'd opened all the way. Having not taken the time to observe whether anyone had been in the elevator car, I crashed right into a chest of drawers. A delayed sting, singed a path through my shoulder.

I grunted, noticing the two large men standing among the furniture pieces that packed the elevator car.

"You okay, miss?" one of them asked.

"Umm-hmm." I couldn't manage any more than that.

The elevator door had closed, taking us to another floor but the next ding of the indicator had come too soon.

"Are you kidding me?" I groaned.

"Excuse me," the other guy said, half hidden by a short case of shelves.

I couldn't wait so I ran out of the car and dashed for the stairs. I shuffled down the steps as fast as my legs would carry me, kicking off my flip-flops mid-stride. Bursting through the lobby doors, breathless and still in a run, I ran for the security counter. I'd been so focused on running I hadn't paid attention to who'd been standing near the rounded desk. I skidded to a halt as Bryant came into focus. He'd been speaking with Gary, who seemed angry. They both turned and looked at me but I whipped around and sprinted in the other direction.

The lobby had always felt big to me, but in this moment it didn't seem big enough. I could not get far enough away from Bryant. The open space left me with nowhere to hide. I looked to either side of me, trying to decide which way to go. Going back upstairs would be horror-movie foolish. I could either run for the front door, which meant I'd have to run pass Bryant or could head for the fire exit.

"Gary, call the police!" I yelled and bolted for the emergency exit.

I reached for the long silver bar, but before I could touch it, someone grabbed me by the ponytail and yanked me back. I heard a crack as my head snapped back, my body crashing onto the marble floor. The impact made a sickening sound which rang in my ears. White and blue flashes of light pulsed in my eyes.

I'd felt so dizzy I thought I'd to see birds circling my head like in the cartoons, but I suppose they were scared shitless as I was and hadn't bothered showing up. While struggling to recapture the wind that had been knocked from my lungs, I peeled my eyes open, trying to distinguish the muffled sounds around me.

"Gary," I coughed out, the lines of his face becoming clearer as I focused on him leaning over me.

He spoke, but I couldn't understand him. Listing my head to the side, I saw Bryant standing in the same place he'd been when I'd burst out of the stairwell.

"Wells...do...think...going," Gary's words faded in and out.

I focused on Bryant for another second. No one else had occupied the lobby except Gary, Bryant and myself and if Bryant hadn't moved, that meant Gary had to have been my assailant. That meant he'd been the one who'd chased me down. That meant the old man who'd been so helpful and sweet to me all this time had just slammed me to the floor. I imagined him as Bruce Banner turning into the Hulk, going from a frail, unassuming man to a beast with unimaginable strength.

"You know, you're more trouble than I thought

you'd be." Each of Gary's words wafted on a breath of air. He'd been so close to my face, I could smell what he'd had for lunch. "I'd hoped getting rid of that nosy husband of yours would be the end of it, but then you decided to pick up where he left off. I guess that means you'll have to suffer the same fate." He turned away from me. "Hey, Bryant, this might even the score!"

I couldn't believe my ears. Gary? Gary had been in on this? He pulled me up by the fistful of hair he'd been clenching in his fist. Once on my feet, he hooked an elbow around my neck, making it even harder for me to breathe. Bryant looked on, his expression carried that of both sympathy and disregard. The latter won out, propelling him toward the elevators and out of sight.

"Bryant!" I cried out.

Even with all I'd learned I still could not fathom him being so heartless.

"Oh, how cute." A sinister grin pulled Gary's face up on one side. "He's not interested in saving you. You know, if you would have just given up the money and heeded the warnings I'd sent you, we could've avoided all this." Gary spoke into my ear.

Despite the utter shock weaving its way through my muscles, it all made sense. Gary had unlimited access to the entire building and could allow anyone entry or hand deliver whatever he wanted without anyone being the wiser. Visions of every unannounced delivery and note floated around my mind, along with the message—*Pop! Pop!*

I shrieked, startled by the loud sound while Gary turned in the direction from which the noise had come.

"Ah," he sneered. "Sounds like my guys are taking care of your little boy toy."

I whimpered, my head throbbed and my legs felt like spaghetti. The elevator dinged and Gary tightened his grip around my neck, dragged me a few feet closer to the exit door and brandished a gun, all at once. He jammed the barrel into my side, spouting orders to me in a hushed voice, threatening to shoot if I tried anything. The steel doors opened and the movers walked out, but I'd noticed something odd. They hadn't unloaded the furniture. The same furniture they'd appeared to be moving onto the fifth floor remained untouched.

"Hello, boys!" Gary sang.

Oh, crap! They're with him! I thought. *This just keeps getting better.* I'd locked eyes with one of the men but out of the corner of my eye, I saw someone else in a far corner of the lobby. Gary, too distracted by his goons, hadn't noticed. When the man who'd hidden himself in the lobby peeked around the corner, I recognized him. Relief inundated every part of me and my legs grew weaker as Santiago pulled himself back into hiding. I tried to be stealthy, to keep from drawing attention to Santiago hunched behind the security desk.

Gary had been preoccupied, speaking to the

moving men in a tone which gave the impression they'd been discussing sports, rather than my life or, in this case, my death. While Gary talked and chuckled I noticed that his southern accent had disappeared.

Santiago peeked out again and motioned for me to get down. I gave a slight nod, even though I had no idea how I'd duck down with a gun in my side. I looked around and one of the fake movers held my eyes again for a moment, but didn't seem too fazed. I felt Gary relax the gun in my side and I used the small window of opportunity and feigned hyperventilation. It hadn't been hard. I'd had enough episodes to be familiar.

"I don't have time for this, Ms. Wells," Gary said in an exasperated tone. "You can die on my time, but that only applies if I have the pleasure of killing you myself."

I crashed down onto my knees so hard it sent a shock of pain through by body. Mere seconds after I'd hit the floor, a gunshot rang out, screaming in my ears. I covered my head with my hands and crouched into a ball. I felt a light kick in my back and heard a thud, then another gunshot shattered the silence. I shrieked again and crawled in Santiago's direction, waiting for a parade of gunfire to follow. It never came.

Santiago swooped me into a pocket of space, blocking me with his body. I saw Gary laid out on the floor and though I couldn't see his face, I did see that his gun was laying a few feet away from him, out of reach. The movers stood over him, guns drawn. I could not understand what had happened but before I could put anything together, cops rushed in through the glass doors. They hadn't arrested the movers as I'd thought they would have, but pat them on the back instead. *What the hell?*

A few minutes later, the elevator doors opened again and out came Bryant and Ali in handcuffs, followed by Trevor. I must have hit my head hard because nothing made sense. A team of paramedics hoisted Gary's inert body onto a gurney, I heard him groan with every shift and jostle.

Santiago stood up, gently pulling me with him.

"Morenita, are you okay? Lo seinto, I wasn't here. I didn't know about Gary until Bryant told me. Did he hurt you?" Santiago's eyes were wild as they roved over me and his hands shook.

The magnitude of all that had occurred smacked me hard just then and I collapsed into his arms. He tucked me under his arm and squeezed my shoulders into him. I'd felt as if I'd wanted to cry, as though I should cry but I couldn't. I hadn't substance. Fear seemed to have arrested my tear ducts.

"Good work, Ruiz." An officer said to Santiago. I'd felt more confused and baffled than ever.

Santiago helped me into a waiting ambulance and climbed in after. They strapped me to gurney, slammed the doors, and whisked us away. Santiago sat alongside me, holding my hand, and humming. He'd never moved his eyes from me, watching as a tear fell from the corner of my eye and pooled in my ear. He wiped my face with the pad of his thumb.

Eleven

alloons, flowers, and cards covered almost every flat surface in the hospital room. Looking around, I tried to sit up but something prevented me from moving. One at a time, I bent each leg and arm but neither would move very far. Not again! Why had they tied me up? I panicked, thrashing around and screaming. I didn't want to do this again. I could not bear to see this again, to live this again.

"Where's Santiago? Where's Santi—" I yelled, desperate and fraught.

"Estoy aquí! Estoy aquí. I'm here. I'm here. I'm here. I haven't left you. Silencio, mi amor. Shh."

The sound of Santiago's voice soothed my soul like a tranquilizer. He hummed and brushed his hand over my hair with one hand and stroked my arm with the other. I relaxed at the touch of his hand, melting with the melody of his soothing song. I pulled my wet lashes apart and gazed at him, hearing the rapid approach of hospital staff adding a drumming beat to his music. Santiago's hand flew up and the beat stopped, freezing them in their tracks. My eyes on him, I got lost in the pool of his eyes. *He's here.* I sighed.

Santiago kissed my nose.

"I'm not leaving you," he reassured, kissing my lips.

He hadn't just kissed me with morning breath, but with funky hospital, morning breath—a far worse thing to endure. He stood up and my eyes grew wide.

"It's okay, it's okay. Don't worry."

He kept one hand in contact with my body, walking around my bed, and then I heard the bed rail squeak. Following that, I felt him climb into bed behind me. I could feel him, hear him, smell him. He felt a lot like love.

On the bedside table, rested a phone, notepad, and pen. I picked up the pen, reached for Santiago's arm and pulled it around my waist, clamping it beneath my arm. Taking his hand, palm up, I wrote: 'Te Amo Tambien' and dropped the pen to the floor. He lifted his hand and read it.

"I know," he said. "I know."

We spent a few days in the hospital, discovering that I'd sustained a concussion, fractured ribs, and a bruised back. While there, I got a surprise visit from Seth, who poked his head just inside the door one afternoon. Shock registered on his face when he saw me. I don't know if it'd been because of how dreadful I might have looked or because of the beautiful attachment who'd been sharing the bed with me, perhaps both.

Bringing his customary bouquet of flowers and sweets, he'd walked over to the bed, speaking to me in hushed tones as though Santiago couldn't hear him. He looked very uneasy, and if it hadn't been apparent before, my lack of interest in him had to be clear.

Seth had stared at me and Santiago for a few minutes, fiddling with his keys before making a quiet exit. Through the window, I saw that he'd stopped and talked to Kennedy. I almost felt bad for him, but other emotions had inundated any sympathy I might have had for Seth.

All my days had run together, and I could not distinguish one from the other. Unable to get a solid grasp of time, I ignored it instead. At a point, Santiago clarified all that had happened concerning Gary, Bryant and Ali.

Gary, he'd explained, had been the ringleader and the founder of the phony companies we'd discovered, along with some others. During his military career as special ops, he'd learned several languages and had acquired the skill to change his identity. The authorities had never caught Gary before, since Ali had been his fall guy, the man had a pristine record. Ali, however, couldn't say the same. He'd taken the heat, done the time, if necessary, and Gary had rewarded him each time. Bryant had just been a tool, a pawn, and my Skylar, a casualty. The list of crimes went on and on, so did the list of victims—dead and alive. Bryant had not known the entire story and had been informed with the necessary information to get his end of the job done, nothing more. When Bryant had gone back upstairs to rejoin Ali, he'd had a flash of conscience, telling Santiago that Gary had hurt and would probably kill me.

The cops had been suspicious about Gary's affiliation with Ali, but hadn't anything on him to warrant an arrest or anything substantial enough to stick. So, they sent Trevor in, hoping to get some evidence or something incriminating to use. While undercover, Trevor had assigned himself as my bodyguard, which explained his overwhelming concern. He'd apprehended Bryant and Ali while Santiago rushed down to me. The movers had been undercover cops as well.

As for Santiago, he had been a bodyguard once upon a time and had toyed with the idea of joining the police force, but never did. That, however, didn't stop him from forming alliances. The files and pictures Skylar had compiled and security tapes from the gallery and the condo lobby had all been seized as evidence. Thinking about the notes, letters, and packages, I hoped they'd found them all. The money everyone had been after—according to investigators—had never existed. Considering the fraudulent activity and crooked "businessmen," trying to track down the cash wasn't a battle worth pursuing as far as they were concerned. They'd caught the bad guys and that seemed good enough.

The unmarked box which, I'm sure, Gary had sent, and I'd never opened, held a single item: Skylar's wedding band. Returned to me, I'd threaded it onto the necklace which also held my wedding ring.

On my final morning in the hospital, a nurse woke me as she checked my vitals again. Santiago lay beside me with his eyes closed, but I knew he wasn't asleep. The nurse gave an empathetic smile.

"He never leaves, does he?" she whispered. "I swear he's a patient too. Should I take his vitals?" She giggled.

I giggled with her, knowing Santiago had been listening. She took my temperature and blood pressure, and then placing her fingers on the inside of my wrist, she monitored my pulse and respirations. The light reflected a tiny glint. At first I didn't pay much attention until I noticed the nurse didn't have any jewelry on, except for a watch on the opposite arm which she held up to her eyes, counting the seconds.

The hospital staff had removed the jewelry I'd had on when they'd admitted me, days before, but I felt a ring on my finger. As I had done many times before, I ran my thumb along the inside of my finger and felt the cool of metal against my warm skin. *When had I put my ring back on?* I didn't remember taking it off my necklace nor did I remember putting it back on finger.

I stretched out my fingers, one at a time until they

were all within view and that's when I saw an undeniable, sparkling, oval cut, bright green diamond. The colored jewel, encircled by a halo of tiny white diamonds on a dainty band flanked with more precious stones, stared at me from my left ring finger. I gasped.

"Is everything okay, Mrs. Ruiz?" The nurse asked. I looked at her, puzzled but she just winked and walked away.

"They can only call you that if you agree to marry me," Santiago said from his simulated sleep.

"Santi..." I began, but I had no other words.

"You're all green, my love." he said.

I imagined my eyes glossy and green, filled to the brim and overflowing with happiness.

Epilogue

On a Sunday morning, the sun had risen over the horizon, washing the room in its apricot radiance. Large industrial windows spanned the wall and the light poured inside. I gazed at Santiago as he slept, his light snore sounding in timed rhythms. His skin had been tinted by the color of sunshine, the glow kissing his cheek and bare shoulder. I'd stared at him for a long moment and then smiled. I'd been such a blessed woman to have, not one great love, but two. I knew he'd wake soon, so we could get ready for church, which we went to most Sundays. Talking in his sleep the night before, I'd heard him say he hadn't deserved me. Funny thing, I hadn't been sure I'd deserved him either.

I'd slid out of bed and tiptoed to the kitchen, surprised my movement hadn't waked him considering he slept so close to me. I'd poured myself a drink, walked over to the window, and pulled the heavy drapes to the side. Surveying the quiet streets below, I realized I couldn't hear Santiago's snore anymore. I smiled around the lip of my glass and a moment later his arms were around my waist. He squeezed me, whispering in my ear.

"Buenos días, mi esposa."

I giggled. We had been married for a little over eight months and still, hearing him call me his wife or anyone else for that matter, sounded foreign to my ears. He always made it sound so good. Then again, he made most things he said in Spanish sound good. I don't know if I cared much about what he'd say to me, so long as he made it sound appealing. Many times he'd talk to me or sometimes reprimand me in Spanish; the words gliding by misunderstood, mollifying me all the same, regardless of their intent. "I love you too." I'd respond, kissing him on the lips. Even amid his annoyance, he couldn't help but be amused.

"I thought you were asleep," I said.

"I was, but then it got really cold in there. My pocketful of sunshine had left me."

He always made me so giddy. How old am I, twelve? I spent the morning in his arms, sunken into the plush cushions of the couch. We'd needed no television nor radio. Sitting there, we talked and laughed as if we didn't spend every day together. We had not spent one night apart since the first time he'd slept at the condo.

At last, we'd made it to church, a little late, having fallen victim to each other's ardor, again. Afterwards, we'd gone to my favorite bookstore in Santa Cruz. Mr. and Mrs.

Kenier loved seeing the two of us together. Our routine remained the same. Santiago would find a corner on the floor, and would sit and watch me gawk, touch, and gaze at rows of books. Sometimes, I'd join him, sitting between his crisscrossed legs. Mrs. Kenier had snapped a photo of us, capturing one of those moments and we hadn't even noticed. In the picture, Santiago's lips were at my ear, a mischievous smile on his face, and I'd been laughing. My hair cascaded towards our knees and an opened book rested in my hands. Mrs. Kenier had sent us a copy of the picture in the mail. She'd insisted we sign up for her old-fashioned mailing list, consisting of postal address rather than emails.

Back at home, the bookshelves which once occupied the condo Skylar and I had shared now decorated the west wall of the loft I lived in with Santiago. Since then, Santiago added additional shelving for my growing collection. He'd built the bookshelves by hand and they stretched from the floor to the ceiling, coming up short by a quarter inch. Books stuffed the openings, but I'd left empty spaces for pictures.

One contained the picture of Santiago and me at the bookstore, others of Kennedy and me, and my favorite picture of Skylar and me sat in its own space. Santiago understood enough not to push me to purge every memory of Skylar. His understanding is one of the things I loved most about him.

My Sundays were a lot different than they used to be, but then again so were Kennedy and Bryant's. Kennedy had divorced Bryant after his sentencing, sold their house, and moved into my condo. She still went to the country club almost every Sunday, but instead of golf, she'd taken a liking to tennis—and the tennis instructor.

Bryant had received a number of years in prison for multiple charges, including money laundering and vehicular homicide. They'd discovered he had international bank accounts used in conjunction with Finge. He had also been embezzling money from the company he worked for, trying to pay off his debts. Gary still awaited sentencing. The authorities were still sorting through his charges and gathering evidence from far away and long ago. It turned out that he'd never been married, nor did he have any children. Ali had been charged with robbery, nothing more. He had managed to evade the heavier charges, despite the implications. He'd posted bail not long after his arrest and vanished.

Monday morning hadn't come as early as the day before, but with the same feeling. I'd kissed Santiago on the lips and eased out of bed. He didn't even stir. I went to the kitchen and poured myself a tall drink of milk and guzzled it down. I poured myself another glass and replaced the carton of milk in the refrigerator. Halfway through the glass of milk, mid-swallow I had an epiphany. The glass slipped from my fingers crashed to the floor. Milk splattered onto my bare feet. In a flash, Santiago appeared next to me. I hadn't even heard his approach.

"¡Mi vida! ¿Qué Pasa? Are you okay?" He all but shouted at me.

I just stood there, motionless. He scooped me up into his arms and rushed me over to the couch, my toes dripping a milky path. He grabbed a towel and dried my feet while rambling under his breath.

"¿Cariño?"

"I need to go to the doctor," I said. "Now."

We arrived at the doctor's office in no time and though Santiago, I'm sure, hoped I'd tell him something, anything, he'd waited without a word. I saw the nurse first, who went through all the routine procedures and then the doctor performed an exam. Once finished, I went into the doctor's private office to speak with her, leaving Santiago in the waiting room.

Dr. Keisha Morgan had been my doctor since I'd moved to California. A beautiful shade of hazelnut, she wore her hair cropped close to her head in tight, wayward curls. With a soothing temperament and inviting eyes, she made me want to tell her my life story, which I may have done. We often spoke as if we were friends rather than patient and doctor.

I stared at her with my mouth agape. I couldn't form any words.

"Definitely?" I choked out.

"Definitely," she said.

I walked out of her office and she'd followed close behind me. I heard the squeaking springs of the couch strain against Santiago's weight as he stood. He looked at my face and then to Dr. Morgan. His expression etched worry into the lines around his eyes and mouth.

"Doctor, what's wrong? Es mi vida okay?" he asked. His nervousness apparent, Santiago mixed languages, unable to stick to one tongue.

"Yes, Mr. Ruiz. She's fine. Echo?" She looked at me, but I remained silent, holding the deer in the headlights look in place on my face.

"Congratulations are in order," she said. "You're having a baby!"

I heard the words aloud and blinked, sending tears I hadn't known were there sliding down my cheeks. Santiago didn't say a word. He looked into my eyes for the confirmation my lips didn't make.

"Mi luz del sol, tú eres todo verde." He wrapped me in his arms and swung me around. I translated in my head before answering him: 'My sunshine, you are all green.'

"Yes. Yes I am." I buried my face in his neck and sobbed. The entire office had become hushed or maybe we'd tuned out the world.

The next few months went by like a cool summer breeze. Santiago brought me breakfast in bed every morning. He'd make a loaded omelet with whole-wheat toast and always brought two tall glasses of milk; the milk always came first. He walked around with a bounce in his step because we had a doctor's appointment and would find out the sex of the baby.

Santiago, over the moon about the pregnancy, had already converted what used to be our office, into a nursery, except for part of the room, which he'd set up for Helena. We had been granted visitation and were pursuing a reasonable custody agreement, hoping to get her for the summers, once she became school aged. We had already made two visits to Colombia, the first for Thanksgiving and the second for Christmas. One look at Helena proved she belonged to Santiago. She looked so much like him that I wondered if Cristina had had anything to do with her creation.

I'd insisted we wait to buy anything for the baby; considering I'd never gotten rid of the gifts I'd received during my first pregnancy. I had not ever imagined this day would come for me again, but some part of me must have known. We had a one o'clock appointment, which we almost didn't make. Somebody got a little frisky, but I won't say which one of us.

We'd rushed in with guilt-ridden faces and the receptionist giggled behind the glass window. Once we were in the dimmed lights of the ultrasound room, we'd, at last, paid attention to someone else besides each other. The technician did the ultrasound first and let us hear the heartbeat, an indescribable and emotional moment for both Santiago and me. Then the tech made a strange face, replacing my awe with fear. Santiago didn't appear to notice, but he'd felt my body tense and looked up.

"What? What's the matter? What's wrong? Is the baby okay?" I asked.

The tech didn't answer right away and the baby's heartbeat, a song to my ears moments ago, all of a sudden, sounded strange. I read the woman's name tag, quelling the desire to scream her name so she'd answer me, so she'd hear me.

"Mi amor, Qué pasa?" Santiago asked.

"I don't know! Wha—" I began, a sense of alarm blaring in my tone.

"Shh, está bien, está bien," Santiago tried to calm me with his Spanish soothings.

"Mr. and Mrs. Ruiz," the tech began. *Oh, so it does speak,* I thought. "I'm going to get Dr. Morgan. Just a moment, please."

She turned on her heel and departed before either of us could demand an explanation. Santiago and I didn't even speak during the wait. Dr. Morgan entered with a bright smile, disarming me on sight.

"My favorite couple, how are you?" she asked.

"Much better if you tell us what's going on," Santiago answered, not as disarmed as me. She began the ultrasound again.

"Well, here's your baby's foot...and hand." She pointed to the formations on the screen. "And here..." She dragged her finger to another dark blur. "Are you sure you want to know the baby's gender?" We nodded. "Here is your baby's penis."

"We're having a boy," Santiago, half stated, half asked. Dr. Morgan nodded. She began again, pointing and identifying one blur after another, but I didn't understand why.

"This arch here is the baby's spine...and this is the arm and this baby seems to be sucking her thumb," she'd stated with a mischievous grin.

"Excuse me?" I asked. "What do you mean she? You just said we were having a boy."

Santiago looked just as perplexed as I did, if not more.

"You are," she said but nothing registered. "You're having a boy and a girl. You're expecting twins."

"¡Aye Dios Mio!" Santiago's knees buckled and he fell into the chair behind him.

He rested his head on my shoulder and I toyed in his hair, flabbergasted. Two babies!

"My love?" I called.

"Sí, mi vida," he answered.

My mouth tilted into a shy grin.

"I'm all green," I said, my joy apparent.

He looked into my glistening eyes and kissed me full on the lips.

"Sí. Yes, you are!"

Return to the stronghold all you prisoners of hope.
Even today I declare that I will restore double to you.
Zechariah 9:12

In loving memory of

Emma "Dear" Thompson

NEFARIOUS

Cavanaugh rolled to his side, still asleep for the most part. He felt the hardwood beneath his body, which meant he'd never moved from the floor and, as a consequence, had slept there. It wasn't the first time it'd happened, and he would wager a hefty bet it would not be the last. He groped for the softness of Sarah among the hard surface without parting his eyelids.

"Seej?" he called into the quiet but received no answer.

This little name he'd given Sarah was a combination of initials. He often teased her about them with lame jokes that riddled him with laughter. Him and no one else. Her initials spelled the word "see." He'd added a "j" for Jones, therefore dubbing her Seej.

He continued to grope the cold, wet sheets where he lay. Wait, why were they wet? Surely he hadn't pissed himself, or had he? He had not been that drunk since college. Perhaps that was the reason Sarah wasn't next to him where she should be. That still didn't explain the wetness...nor the stickiness.

Cavanaugh, his eyelids crusted together with the evidence of sleep, forced his eyes open. He needed to inspect what his fingers were touching. Taking the back of his hand, he rubbed one eye, trying to remove some of the goo so he could see. Opening his eyes in stages, he winced at the brightness of the sun as it washed the dark paint of his bedroom walls. Straining to focus on the pillow where Sarah should be laying, Cavanaugh cast his eyes downward expecting to see her wrapped in the tangle of sheets. His breath caught on an inhale.

"Wha—?" His voice came out in a low whisper, scratchy and thick.

In a frantic flail of hands and feet, Cavanaugh pushed the sheets away from him. He wrestled with the covers that blanketed him, trying to extract himself, all the while sliding backwards on the floor, away from the horrific vision he hoped was a nightmare. Could he still be asleep? He hoped to God he was. Although he'd never believed in all that holy mumbo jumbo, if any of it were true, he didn't want to dismiss it now. God, please let me be dreaming, he thought, not wanting to hear his own voice again.

He continued to slide for what felt like an infinite

distance until his back slammed into a bookcase against the wall. The shelves, filled with Sarah's girlie magazines, notebooks, and puzzles banged and rattled, shaking its books loose from their perches. One of her beloved puzzle books fell beside Cavanaugh as he stared, mouth agape, at the vision that it seemed he wasn't going to wake up from.

The pastel colored, floral sheets had been saturated, stained a sickening shade of red, while the smell of iron permeated the air. In his effort to flee—a feeble attempt, at best—Cavanaugh had streaked the substance across the floor where it ended on the spot where he sat. He looked around in confusion and disbelief, wondering where the blood had come from.

 DSEANBOOKS.COM

Acknowledgements

I would first like to acknowledge my mother who provided the stimuli that would morph into the inspiration that formed these words into a story. Thanks for allowing me to stay up past my bedtime reading books by the glow of a nightlight...the types of books I would one day write. I thought I'd been clever, but I knew better than to think I'd get away with something... anything, and so did she.

Secondly, I want to give great thanks to my editors Cheryl P. Brown and TJ Walp for all their hard work. Thanks for smoothing out the fabric of this novel so that it may become an even more enjoyable read. I appreciate Cheryl for encouraging my dreams over the years. As for TJ, she is stellar! That's the only way I can sum her up.

My final acknowledgment, but one that bears no less weight than those before it, is to my peers. To those who listened as I counted up the pages and read them even before I knew what to do with them. Special thanks to Miasha for plugging me into all the right outlets, making the transition from manuscript to book much easier. Lisa, for being my own personal cheerleader. Katina, for being a living version of the information highway. Finally, much thanks to those who made contributions to help transform this from an unknown work of fiction into a published work for the masses.

I know I said that was my final acknowledgement but there is one more that can't go without mention. To all the great Loves that I've been blessed with, who unwittingly inspired this story.